The Village at the Riverbend

(Citizens and nomads)

A novel by

Matti Aikio

Translated by John Weinstock

Copyright © 2014 Agarita Press
Dripping Springs, Texas
ISBN-978-0-9907661-0-0

Set in Adobe Jensen Pro

The original of this book was published as

Bygden på Elvenesset
Roman
Forlagt av H. Aschehoug & Co.
(W. Nygaard) ♦ Oslo 1929

Cover art by John Weinstock and Beth Brotherton

**Ollu giitu dáid olbmuide hui buori veahki ovddas:
Reidar Rødland, Harald Gaski, Britt Rajala,
Kikki Jernsletten ja Liv Astrid Kvammen Svaleng.**

**This translation has been published with
the financial support of NORLA.**

Woodcut images from *John Andreas Savio. An Exhibition of His Selected
Works in Texas, Washington and Alaska*. Savio Art Museum, Kirkenes,
1993. For more information on John Savio and Matti Aiko see the last
printed pages.

The Village at the Riverbend

Gánda ja Nieida
Sámi Couple

Hendrik Hooch ran a business in the Sámi and Kven village far inside the country, by a river that came from the southwest, and that more than ten miles below the village ran into another river coming directly from the south that formed the border between the kingdom of Norway and Russian-governed Finland.

Hendrik Hooch's father, in spite of his eighty years, still ran the family's old business in a little coastal town that lay on the north side of the large fjord to the east. The business had once been a firm in the proper sense; now it had shrunk into a store and two or three polar vessels. But the Hoochs were still Hoochs; they had been up here a couple hundred years.

The first Hooch dated back to a Dutch sloop that had been transported up here by one of the Bergen Hanseatic merchants who at that time had a monopoly on the trade up there at the old exile location. An administrative officer wrote in 1778: 'Since they have too many young women and men in the prison in Copenhagen, some of them could be sent here so that the land could be built up and settled.'

And the surplus women and men in the prison in Copenhagen and other places came and fulfilled their calling with dignity and good humor beneath God's open northern lights.

But the first Hooch was an honorable young seaman on the Dutch sloop, and he willingly settled down up here.

◆

Hendrik Hooch, the merchant in the Sámi and Kven village in the interior of the country, had in his younger days once attempted violin and medicine in Christiania, yet mostly Bacchus and Venus. But when the handsome young man one spring morning in the sun and south wind woke up to a melancholy consciousness, he said in appalling sincerity to himself: "Lord, teach me to number my days!"

7

And the year after he ended up as a merchant here, far from the sea, with desolate mountain plateaus and desolate valleys in between. He married a strong and beautiful woman. She was one of the descendants of the women and men who had once been sent here from Copenhagen and other places, that the land could be built up and settled. In the beginning these people were somewhat immoral in their life, stole a little and sinned in many ways. But one or another of them worked themselves up and became proud, some of them became cultured people, and to these belonged Adriane Hooch; some older people thought it most correct to call her Madame.

Hendrik Hooch bought skins and meat and ptarmigans and other wild game, had a number of storehouses outside his large, three story home. In the store he also had a liquor trade and pouring; in the winter there were always a few reindeer Sámi standing at the counter drinking shots, and they yoiked and sang heathen songs. But others, especially the settled Sámi farmers in the southwestern portion of this beautiful village on a river headland on the south side of the river, considered themselves too good to stand there at the counter and drink shots and sing heathen songs. In the glass cabinet at the counter shone gilded pillars and brass rings, and brass rings were so good for people who had rheumatism in their fingers; an old Sámi woman went around with three such rings on each of her ten fingers. And on her shelves lay silk shawls and other textiles in resplendent blue and yellow and green colors. Now and then a reindeer Sámi comes in and tosses a frozen reindeer steak up on the counter: "A couple shots of cognac for that, *Hooká!*"

Hendrik Hooch sent a long string of reindeer and sleds over the plateau in a northwesterly direction; it was 80 miles to the marketplace and the harbor at the bottom of the fjord to the west. And after a week and a half the string came back with sacks of flour and sugar and coffee and other wares.

But the settled Sámi had another winter route over the plateau that went straight northward to a fjord bottom there, and it was only 40 miles; horse caravans went there and returned with Russian flour in sacks of 18 stones, and had with them among other things iron and steel from which they forged scythes and knives.

And there was yet another winter road, eastward down the valley, mostly along the national border, to the mouth of the river or to the village on the fjord to the east.

The grassy hillsides far into the country are full of large fir forests, and most of the river headlands of birch woods. Good God, how the meadows and outlying fields can swell with flowers and grass in rain and the summer's ever-present sun.

And Hendrik Hooch gathered flowers and herbs, he collected stones and minerals; this had become a great, joyful passion for him, and during the summer he was often with Sámi farmers who with their fine, slender river boats poled up the rapids way up the river and fished for salmon.

It may be said that Hendrik Hooch was a happy man.

***

And just before Christmas, preparations for a wedding were made at Hooch Manor, *Hooká* Manor as the Sámi call it. It is Hooch's only daughter, Andijn, who is to get married, to the young attorney Einar Asper. Asper is expected today or at the latest tomorrow, from the town by the fjord. Hooch and his wife have not seen him before. Andijn got engaged to him last spring when she was down in Christiania for the first time in her life. And now in September Asper had settled down as a lawyer in the town on the fjord to the east.

The women, with extra assistance from the sheriff's farm, are in restless activity. The minister has gotten leave and has traveled south with his family; but the substitute curate and his young wife are expected up here one of these days, in any case before Christmas.

Hendrik Hooch has sought refuge in his little, private room up on the second floor and has taken to rummaging around in his drawers and hiding places to calm himself … if only Fridtjof too could come home now! Fridtjof is his only son. Fridtjof is in Archangel to learn Russian and besides is employed at a business there; the idea is that he will take over grandfather's business in the town by the fjord next autumn … No, Hooch can't help it; the thought of Fridtjof always makes him a little uneasy. It isn't only the constant requests for money, no, it's a lot more … Fridtjof was in his way a character, and a fine, strapping boy he was, a real Hooch, but he had some difficult peculiarities … God spare the poor boy too great disappointments in this uncertain world; it was almost as if Fridtjof was created to go from one disappointment to another … At such small moments Hendrik Hooch usually sought a turn for the better in remembering his own youth; when he woke up that melancholy spring morning in Christiania. "Lord, teach me to number my days!" The biblical passage had agreed with him very well at the time; he had even thought of having it framed, and now he wondered whether he should write about it to Fridtjof; but that would perhaps be tempting fate, since history, fate, never repeats itself in this world, and scriptures are so difficult to tamper with.

He gets out the case with the silver medallion from His Majesty Oscar II; he wants to wear it on his chest on Andijn's wedding day. He received it in recognition for having sent so many valuable things to the university's collections: herbaria, mineral stones, old coins and silver and gold items that centuries ago had been brought up here by Kurdish travelers all the way from Moscow and that had been in wealthy reindeer Sámi's possession until recently. And ten years ago, in 1872, Hendrik Hooch had had the honor of arranging His Majesty's journey over the isthmus from the bottom of the fjord to the east and down to the river mouth. It was in *Morgenbladet*; Hendrik Hooch took out the yellowed issue and read it piously.

◆

Yes, everything is basically ready now. Andijn's fiancé, the young attorney Einar Asper, is expected today. He could already have been here this morning; but of course it is 175 miles from the town up to here. He was going to ride a horse the entire way, he wrote in the letter Andijn got in the mail a few days ago.

Today is the 18th of December, and it is almost an entire month since the sun appeared for the last time on the sheltered mountain ridge to the south, above the wooded slopes. But there is a little daylight all the same, at noon.

All the time Andijn has to go out on the steps and look down the main road in the village, listen for whether she might hear the sound of those sleigh bells that the Kvens in the town to the east used. She was familiar with the sound of these sleigh bells from that time when she went to school in the town and lived with her grandparents.

She stands listening: bell sounds are heard from all directions, from the ice on the river that turns around the flat, three-sided headland. The Hooch farmstead lies quite near the riverbank on the headland's lower edge; and from the wooded slopes bell sounds are also heard, but it wasn't the sleigh bells she was listening for.

Even in this dusky daylight her hair shines golden – 19 years old, and so tall; one thought or another makes her smile, and her two upper front teeth come into view. She has a Hooch nose, high too at the base and a bit crooked.

Andijn was born and grew up here in this village of Sámi farmers and reindeer Sámi; so she surely can distinguish the sound of the sleigh bells that are used here from the sound of those that are used in the town. Indeed, she knows the sound of every single sleigh bell in the village.

Mother opens the front door.

"You mustn't stand here so uncovered, my child; at least put a fur coat on if, by all means, you are going to stand here."

Andijn goes in. It's not more than two o'clock; but it is already almost dark.

"Should we light the inside lights, mother?"

"The inside lights? We won't do that until we hear him come."

"But if Einar came driving without our hearing it in time? It would be so pleasant with lights in all the rooms."

Mother is silent a while.

"Oh, we'll have enough time to light the lights when we hear the sleigh bells."

And Andijn has to go out again and listen, listen. She has put on a fur coat; but she is a little cold where she is standing on the steps. A distant sound of sleigh bells – she starts, listens and holds her breath; but the sleigh bell sound died away. Maybe it was just a whistle in her expectant ears.

Mother opens the front door.

"You must understand that a horse ride does not run on a schedule."

"No, I know that. But there has been no problem with the road conditions this week."

Mother goes in; but Andijn remains on the steps.

The air is calm under the chilly, clear sky. And now the northern lights begin to cascade down in incredible quantities. Light, immensely high and brilliantly colored waterfalls of cold, transparent fire right up there beneath the heaven's stars, and the reflection goes over the snow land down here.

Finally, Andijn goes in. Her mother sees that she is pale. And Andijn goes out again, to get hold of the hired man, a Sámi boy, who is the handyman here on the farmstead.

"Will you go down to the riverbank below the village, Lasse, and stand there until you hear the sleigh bells. When you know or see the transport come driving up over the ice, run right back and tell us."

And Lasse rushed down. He was just as absorbed by all this as the master and mistress of the household themselves.

An hour passed, then another. And no Lasse appeared. The supper table was set. Hooch and his wife sat down to eat, but not Andijn.

But Hooch and his wife ate just for appearance's sake.

Finally, Lasse came; but he had nothing to report and he looked like it was his fault that he had nothing to report.

Andijn put on her outer clothes and went out.

Hooch and his wife sit alone in the living room. They try to say a word or two, in strained silence. But they constantly discover that they are sitting silently. Then Hooch gets up and says with a voice that quivers with scornful bitterness:

"This is just damn nonsense, this behavior of Andijn! She is making us depressed too! I'll swear that Asper doesn't come before the day after tomorrow, at the earliest!"

"Yes, that could really happen that he doesn't arrive before then," his wife says relieved.

"And if besides there had been something wrong then he would, of course, have sent an extra messenger here. One must assume that he is a well-bred man."

"For quite a while, Andijn has been gone," his wife says.

Lasse was sent to the sheriff's farmstead. No, she wasn't there. And the parsonage that lay right in front of the Hooch farmstead was empty at present.

Andijn is standing on the riverbank at the lower end of the headland, where the winter road leads down onto the ice in the river, only to again go up onto the next headland on this side, on the south side. She is not able to look up at the living and fleeing and hurrying silk blankets of yellow and red and green light up there beneath the heaven's stars. She sees only the reflection on the ice and river, must see it because it goes over the road that Einar will come on and that her glance is fixed on. The weakest sound of distant bells causes her to be startled; it whistles in her ears, and even if it only sounds like the sound of sleigh bells, it is, even so, like a real sound. And if it just seems like someone is driving down on the ice from the headland below, then it is a vision that is difficult to get rid of.

Andijn goes down the hill and down onto the snow-covered ice. A long row of birch twigs are planted in the ice on both sides of the road.

"Andijn!"

Andijn stops and turns.

It is her father who comes running after her.

◆

What good does it do to turn in bed, when one cannot sleep anyhow? No, it doesn't help, that's for sure; but you turn anyway, something you have to do. And occasionally Andijn lies listening, listening. The light from the night's frosty clear sky is camped in front of her two windows to the east. If only she hadn't come to think about it, the one … But now she has become a helpless victim of this nightmare of a thought. Yesterday morning she was happy at the sight of her lovely limbs and beautiful breasts because the day, her day, was so near. Now she is holing herself up and doesn't think about it any more; she has only the one bad thought to struggle with.

◆

And morning came, and day, but no sleigh bells to be heard. And now dusk again.

◆

Andijn and her father sit alone in the living room. Her father now sees, what his wife had already seen in the morning, that the expression in Andijn's eyes seemed to threaten to want to lose hold of itself. And the whole house besides seems to be filled by a suffocating idea. Now something has to be said, at all costs. And Hooch says:

"Andijn … I have to tell you something …"

Andijn gets up, with a feverishly burning countenance.

"Yes, just say it, father! Say it, whatever it is!"

Hooch clears his throat a little.

"Your fiancé, Einar Asper, is not at this moment in control of his own freedom of movement."

"Not in control?"

"No, for I unfortunately have reason to fear that he has embezzled money or some such."

Andijn's face becomes clear. It clears into a bright smile:

"Oh, not worse! So he has been in danger, poor thing! … Oh, not worse! … Father! I will be faithful to him too in his humiliation. I will, father! Otherwise, I would be a poor, bad person!"

And Andijn suddenly and really seems to betray a sort of happy feeling.

"But what sort of embezzlement has he done, the poor thing?"

Hooch couldn't hit upon anything for the moment, but said was said, and he had seen Andijn's face brighten, heard her voice sound relieved. He had to continue as he had begun:

"Yes, it's probably some trust funds, that …"

"Yes, that's probably it. But they say that that sort of thing happens, even with people who otherwise are not bad people. And it is perhaps quite excusable. Yes, sad of course, one loses ones good name and reputation, perhaps for good. Oh, I'll be good to Einar nevertheless! Never, never, will I betray him!"

Goodness, how Andijn sounded wise and good!

And late in the evening she sits on the edge of the bed and is happy. Yes, for it was after all not the dreadful thing. What she had begun to think about the previous night. And it was just the one thing that was the only dreadful thing that there could perhaps be another … Oh, now the thoughts are going again; seasickness comes …

And again it is morning, and it becomes day. But no sleigh bells to be heard. And it gets dark.

And again Andijn and her father are sitting alone in the living room. Hooch isn't able to look at his daughter any more. Something has to be said again, at all costs. He knows, understands what the one dreadful thing is for Andijn. He says:

"I have to confide one more thing to you, Andijn."

"Yes, just say it, father! And if it is something ghastly, so much the better?"

"There has been mental illness in your fiancé's family."

"Mental illness? Is that true!"

"Yes, and I have heard that Asper has a tumor on his brain."

"Oh, is that true! … Poor Einar!"

And now Andijn's countenance again appears to brighten. She gets up.

"Have you really heard that, father! Is it really true?"

"Yes. And now you must not become too dismayed, dear child. But it is possible that the tumor has worsened during the trip."

Andijn gets up and looks at her father with wide-open eyes.

"Do you really think so, father?"

"Yes, something like that must have happened. One thing or another must have caught up with him."

Andijn stands staring straight ahead. Then she smiles, almost happy.

"But I don't want to fail him. I want to be good to him! I want to care for him. I will be faithful to him until death … Yes, for then he will probably die, the poor thing."

And Andijn's voice again sounds silvery, although it quivers, sincerely and moved. And she sits down, remains sitting so quietly. The tension in her mind seems to have subsided and a great, tired calm has settled on her face.

"I think I want to go up and lie down. I feel so tired and sleepy."

"Yes, go up and lie down, Andijn."

And Andijn goes up.

14

A moment later his wife comes into the kitchen. Hooch dreads telling her what wool he has tried to pull over Andijn's eyes. But it has to be told.

"I couldn't do anything else. She is threatened by the worst, the poor thing. God forbid that the remedy I have been forced to have recourse to will not lead to a too fateful end."

His wife is sitting and crying.

"It's good that Fridtjof is not at home. Yes, for you know how Fridtjof is. Nothing could have prevented him from getting terribly violent with Asper."

But now Hooch loses his temper.

"But I say: would that Fridtjof had been home!"

And before Hooch knew it he had gotten into a terrible rage. He grabs a chair and bangs on the ceiling with it.

"Andijn! Come down immediately!"

Andijn comes running down, tense.

"Is he coming?" she asks with an excited look.

"Coming? No, damn it, he isn't! But now I tell you, Andijn, he'll come anyway, tomorrow or later, but there's one thing I know, he is not going to come into this house – as sure as I'm alive! He is not going to get a glimpse of you!"

Andijn stands there holding her breath; in a jiffy the word has flared up. That word she herself was unable to find an outlet for and didn't dare admit; ignored it and excused herself by being tempted to think so evilly and simply because she was suffering, suffering so very much. In a sort of mild and relieved tone she says:

"But of course he could have had serious obstacles, obstacles that he wasn't able to deal with, and then you know …"

But she can't conceal that her father's violent utterance has given her a solution; in a fleeting, flush moment she became intoxicated with this violent notion: Her father standing on the steps and waving Einar Asper off, without forgiveness – that's that.

Hooch is trembling.

"For either the man is crazy or too he is a shameless cad who gets a despicable kick out of doing this sort of thing. The one is no better than the other – forgive me, but it will not happen that he sets foot inside my doorstep!"

"But father! … If it turned out that he didn't have control over …"

"Control over? Whatever has been going on he surely could have sent a message up here. He is – I'll be damned – not worthy to get a whipping even, a kick in the behind is the only thing one can offer that fellow!"

Andijn goes up to herself; but first she slips out on the steps and listens a little. … Then she sits alone in her room. If he comes now, oh, everything would be forgotten! And father would also surely be himself again. The clock on the wall ticks, and now Andijn becomes a victim of her own inner vision of the other side: father stands on the step waving Einar Asper off, without forgiveness, that's that. And had Fridtjof been here, he would not have been satisfied waiting. He would have hitched up and driven down, Fridtjof with his blind need for self-assertion! Einar is probably a fine and dignified gentleman to look at, but would surely be completely insignificant if he was subject to injustice of that sort. … Yes, for gentlemen with his fine manners cannot be conceived in such a situation. Andijn remembered from Karl Johan last spring, a customer could distinguish a noted gentleman from others at a long distance. It was this somewhat relaxed attitude and gait; and Einar had just such an attitude and gait.

Hooch's mind had calmed down. And it is already late in the evening. Hooch and his wife are sitting in the living room, apathetically silent.

Suddenly a powerful noise of sleigh bells is heard. Andijn comes running down the steps, throws the door open.

"Light the lights!" … And she goes up again. But even before Hooch and his wife have gathered their wits to undertake something, the sleigh bells are already quite near. They remain standing as if paralyzed by excitement, by confusion. It could be him after all! But in a jiffy everything went past. It was probably just one or another Sámi farmer out on a sleigh ride with his sweetheart.

It was like a locked silence that had stuck a key into itself. … A little later Andijn comes down, slowly, quiet, and says with sorrowful, wide-open eyes:

"Turn out the lights!"

"We didn't light the lights," her mother says.

"No? Good. And don't light the lights any more, even if a hundred sleigh bells are heard! I will immediately turn off my own lamp. And go now and go to bed and turn off the lamp you too! And lock the door! And don't open it up, if – yes, if it happened that he came."

And she goes up.

But Hooch and his wife remain sitting there with the locked silence between them. Sit there a long time, long time.

Now a little, gentle sound of an ordinary horse bell is heard. The sleigh runners and the horseshoes squeak heavily and tediously against the hard packed frosty snow outside. It is probably a cargo sled out so late. The squeaking sound becomes silent outside here. It becomes a death silence also here in the living room. And Andijn doesn't come down. The outer front door is opened, they hear. There is a somewhat clumsy knock on the door, and in steps a Sámi in a huge and heavy, longhaired reindeer coat, and with a rimed, red wool scarf on his neck. He takes off his otter skin cap. The crown is wide and square and filled with down.

"*Buorre eahket* – good evening," he says.

"*Ipmel atti* – may God grant!" Hooch says. They speak in Sámi. "Well, well, it's you."

Hooch knew *Oula Oula* well, Ole Olsen. He was from a group of farms on the river 100 miles from here, where the river forms the border to Finland. Hooch and his wife immediately understood what errand the man had. *Oula* says:

"The attorney didn't think he could wait until the mail got up here and so he sent me off with the documents."

He drew the ends of the inner sash of the coat lining, found the letters and handed them to Hooch.

Hooch didn't put any questions to him; he just took the letters and asked his wife to take *Oula* with her into the kitchen and give him some food.

No, Andijn didn't come down.

One of the letters was for Andijn. But he didn't want to send it up to her before he had read the one that was to him.

◆

"Mr. Hendrik Hooch.

Dear Andijn's father,

Yes, already when I was driving inward along the fjord on Sunday I began to have an uneasy feeling, even if quite uncertain, that this road and goal for my trip had begun to become so unreal and strange to me. But I dismissed the thoughts and tried to explain it to myself in this way that there were perhaps other concerns that had put me in a bad mood. I drove over the isthmus, came down into the valley, drove a few miles up to the sheriff's farm in P. No, I didn't stop there, since I was simply afraid that I would stop there too long and give my absurd notions force. I therefore drove on, and out into the night I eventually reached the little, decently cared for Sámi farm a few miles above *Storsluget*, the Big Chasm (that was now under large blocks of ice). And here at Ellen's it is good enough for cultured people to find lodging.

Now I don't know for sure what I should tell first, and what I should tell last. But I think it is best that I take it in chronological order. You will then more easily understand what this letter must end with.

I'm an old horseman, and I therefore ride alone; I just rented a horse from a Kven in the town and rode away. Now, I arrive at Ellen's whom I have heard spoken of as an excellent Sámi woman. I unhitch and go in through an unlocked door; there were still embers in the fireplace, and Ellen comes down from the attic room in loose Sámi slippers, a little sleepy, but with a gentle and loving expression on her face. 'Hello,' I said, 'you are Ellen, isn't that so?'

'Yes,' and she says: 'Perhaps you are the prefect curate, and are going up to the inland village to substitute for the minister who has traveled to the south?'

It is in vain to try to explain the following; I only know that it was just nothing but in jest that I answered: 'Yes.' And I cannot reproach myself enough.

Ellen's face brightened, and with an unusually good and heartfelt smile she takes me by the hand and says: 'Well, welcome to the minister. I myself am from up there, and therefore I feel that the minister has somehow come to us.'

Oh, what a pure and good expression in her pure, lovely face with the beautiful blue eyes. And now the serious stuff begins. My impression of her had surprised me, and I – yes, I must try to explain it to myself in this way – I was somehow unable to disappoint her right away and say that I was not the curate, but the attorney Einar Asper. In any case, I had to wait a little I thought, and the joke was also tempting. And right afterwards her husband Per comes down, also in loose Sámi slippers; he had heard Ellen's and my conversation, and piously and completely trusting he stretches out his hand and says: 'Well, welcome, minister!' I mumbled 'thanks,' confused, without being able to kill my 'joke,' that besides was no longer a joke for me, since I felt paralyzed although I still hadn't lost my conviction that I should rectify the whole thing as soon as we had gathered our wits. 'But your horse must go into the stall,' Per says, and he goes out to take care of it.

Ellen stokes up the fireplace and lights the paraffin lamp hanging over the table below the upper window, and goes into the small side room to light a fire with nice birch wood in the iron stove there.

'And you do not have your wife with you?' Ellen asks. 'No,' I answered. 'But she will be coming later?' 'Yes,' I answered, in a haze, bewildered. Here I must remember again what is at the beginning, that already during the journey along the fjord I had begun to be addicted by a dread that I shall return to, and that the journey and goal of it had begun to turn out as something unreal and strange for me. It would perhaps have been a greater strain than I until now had suspected.

Ellen served all the best dishes she knew and indeed she had all the praise for her effort. I ate delicious boiled reindeer tongue and ice cream. And after a good cup of strong coffee I stuffed tobacco in my long pipe. Oh, how I could have been happy now! … But … no, I wasn't happy … I looked at the shining clean sheepskin blanket and at the reindeer hide that had been laid over the base of soft, fine birch twigs. I had never lain more securely in any bed in the farming country than in this one.

'Well, now the minister can go to bed when he desires,' Ellen says.

Now, I thought, now you must act and free yourself from this nightmare, say it jocularly with my lungs full of pent-up laughter, that things aren't as they seem, I am not the minister. But a glance at Ellen's and her husband's sincere, honest, indeed unaffected and loving faces finished it for me. I was rendered impotent; I was, to speak bluntly, a helpless coward at this moment. Now, I would probably be in a better mood when I had been able to get some sleep … No, I will not try to describe this night, perhaps the worst I've spent in my life.

In the morning, Ellen came in to me with coffee and said that there was a man in the living room who wished to speak with the minister. 'What does he want of me?' I asked. 'He has a little fourteen-day-old child at home who is sick, and he wants to ask whether the minister could be so kind as to come to him and baptize the child, for he is afraid it is going to die.' Merciful God! Now I was in a kettle of fish! And this wasn't the right psychological moment to wind up the prank. I'm not clear as to what I answered Ellen, but I surely said that I was sick. But I remember that the man came in; it was a poor looking Sámi farmer, and he looked troubled and beseeching at me and asks if he in any case couldn't be allowed to bring the child here, then I could baptize it while I lay in bed.

Now I dare say that I have never been addicted to lying, and cowardice has until now been somewhat contrary to my nature. But now without further ado I hit upon a white lie. I answer the man that baptism at home should preferably be done by a layman; didn't they have a teacher who could do it? No, not now at this time of year. Well, then Per, Ellen's husband, can do it. The poor Sámi went away disappointed but comforted.

Well, I couldn't remain lying here and allow myself to die as a wretched man. And remember, dear Hendrik Hooch, that I also had other things pressing me, even more than what was described here, although this was my great difficulty for the present.

I got up and ate mechanically the excellent breakfast Ellen served me. I smoked my pipe for a long time and thought that things were beginning to brighten in my mind. Better to jump in rather than creep in, I thought, and before I realized it I stood there and laughed, well, I desperately mimicked a sort of laughter and said to Ellen: 'Ellen, dear Ellen, I have probably played too coarse a prank – I'm not the prefect curate; I am attorney Einar Asper from the town.' And my eyes looked desirously and disconsolately for a smile on Ellen. I would have given much money for some laughter from her now, at this moment. But there was no indication of a smile on her face; she just stood and looked at me with her strong, honest eyes and said nothing, nothing.

'Can you forgive me, Ellen?' I asked. She did not answer, turned away and tackled her own tasks.

'Can you really not forgive me, Ellen? I have acted so dumb. Are you mad at me, Ellen?'

Then she turned toward me and said: 'No … no, I am not mad at you.' But she said this very seriously.

Her husband, Per, came in, and I felt like the poor school child called to account.

'The gentleman says that he is not the minister,' Ellen says, 'he is an attorney, he is the one who is going to marry Andijn.'

I begged for a smile from the man, yes, I tried also to smile a bit; but Per just cast a serious, disappointed glance at me and turned away.

'Dear Per, I have joked too coarsely. You must forgive me. You must not be too angry with me! Otherwise, I will be very unhappy.' After a while's silence Per says: 'No, when you are not the minister, then you are not the minister.'

✦

And now I must in God's name come to what hurts me so indescribably to have to say; but it is not to be avoided. And what comes now is just for you, dear Hooch.

With my hand on my heart I can take the Almighty as witness that what I tell here happened against my most honest will. Had Andijn been in the town with her grandparents this fall, been close to me, in other words, I would, I hope, quite surely have been able to salvage my love for her! But Andijn and I have in reality been all too little together, and I have not been able to defend myself against the times that have passed, and the distances, the endless distances, that have such a strange ability unwittingly to blow away ones feelings. And I have not been alone by myself in the meanwhile …

In my letter to Andijn today I have given another explanation, namely, that with good reason I have begun to fear that I had gotten a tumor on my brain – Hooch gives a start – and that I therefore had to turn back and hurry to the south to be examined and possibly undergo an operation. And I want to say straight off: I really will travel to the south too. It is a large sacrifice for a man in my economic situation. But Andijn's spiritual wellbeing is well worth that sacrifice, since she thereby will see for herself that it is serious and not just a neat alibi on my part. And I dare furthermore confide in you, in that I blindly rely on your discretion, that it is at the same time really necessary for me to undertake this journey also for another reason, namely that I have an economic obligation down there, which I cannot take care of from here. And a further failure of the arrangement would bring me into a fatal situation."

Here Hooch had to get up; he scratched his head and swore in an overwhelming astonishment at the thought of what he at a guess had dared to say to Andijn. "I myself have never been so far north; but my parents were of course, as you know, from these districts. Yes, Hoochs and Aspers have almost been close relatives once upon a time. And the Asper name must not get a stain.

And finally, I beseech you, dear, noble Hooch, keep this from Andijn! She will probably sooner or later find out about this; but then she will hopefully have already gotten through the worst. That which for the present will be the one terrible thing for her:

Yes, that an earlier girl friend of mine, I can gladly give you her name: Signe André she is called, came up here a month ago to our town as a telegraph operator, absolutely without any cause on my part. If she has had any thoughts about me when she decided to travel I cannot say; women are so very secret in that sort of thing. She and I have naturally been together a lot in these weeks; but notice, dear Hooch, that I nevertheless decided to travel up to you and Andijn, and did so. So there has been a deep sincerity with me.

No, it was only during the trip that I was taken by surprise, by that which I can no longer control. And now my journey stops here; I can't help it. I implore the merciful God that you are successful in concealing what for Andijn would be the worst, the terrible thing, and that will strike her at her point of honor. Besides I have my strong doubts that it will amount to anything with 'that spirit.' When I have spoken about her at all here it is mostly to forestall possibly appearing rumors.

It is still 100 miles up to you, and it is 75 miles back to the town. Here I am. It is a long time since we saw the sun; here there is a touch of color. I know that your village is beautiful and heavily wooded, but here it's desolate and just birch. I'm weighed down by darkness and by all that is lonely and wretched around here. And I am weighed down by my own lack of resoluteness at this moment. I have been here for three days. Ellen and Per and the neighbors look silently and seriously at me; they surely understand that something is the matter with me. They don't even ask when I intend to travel further up; they probably suspect that I will turn back. And then my deeply humiliating faux pas. Well, I've told you that at the beginning of this letter. I'm leaving a letter for the parish chaplain.

A couple hours later.

Now I am sending old *Oula Oula*, Ole Olsen, up to you.

Yours in desperation
Einar Asper."

***

Andijn had received the letter that was for her almost indifferently, half as if it didn't concern her any more, and as if she was no longer in this world. Her kind nature had armed her with an almost unreasonable coolness.

Then she reads the letter, and well being gushes through her. She lays the letter aside without reading it again. She almost has compassion for him; in any case, she is almost eternally thankful that it was nothing other than a sad accident. So many evil, vengeful thoughts that had blended into her painful, burning desire these days! Now she was rid of them. Poor Einar! May it not turn out too bad for him!

✦

The next day, which was Sunday, the postman's horn blew in the wooded hillside to the north, and now came the large postal string of eight reindeer and two men. It came from the marketplace by the fjord bottom to the west, 110 miles from here, over the mountain plateau.

Just a small fraction of the mail was for the village here, some Christmas packages for the Hoochs and the sheriff, and a couple local newspapers from the county here and a couple newspapers from Trondheim, and then *Morgenbladet* for the minister. But there were no less than nine large postal sacks of dark leather and with solid locks and handles. They were going to the villages and a couple towns on the fjord furthest east. For in the times this report is derived from, a postal boat, the Hamburg boat, as it was called, went just once in the winter to the east. The lighter mail was brought weekly over the inner part of the land.

It was Hanas Ommuk and Anne Ommuk who had their turn this time. Hanas Ommuk was a Sámi farmer. But he was married to the daughter of a reindeer Sámi and could take the responsibility for mail delivery. He was a man of means, a Swedish count in reindeer coat to look at – there was hardly a drop of Sámi blood in him; but a Sámi he was, as so many non-Sámi here and elsewhere.

It was Hooch who was the mail opener here. Early this morning he had written a short and pithy letter to Einar Asper. He was already about to lock the mailbag when Andijn came with a letter to Mr. Einar Asper.

"No, don't talk about it, Andijn! The message I have given him is enough. That's that!"

And Hooch locked the mailbag.

Here the mailbags were put up into two large horse sleds, and Andijn had the opportunity to hand her letter to one of the mail drivers.

But afterwards she regretted that she had written so warmly and so bitterly. And then she was again satisfied that she had written so warmly and so bitterly.

Lotka
Stillness

Not until the night before Christmas Eve did the district curate arrive here, and he could tell – what also old Oula Oula who had brought the letters had done before – what a depressing impression attorney Einar Asper had made on Ellen and Per in the little group of farms down there. And it wasn't just the Hoochs who got to hear. Everyone in the village got thorough information on the poor attorney, so Andijn and her parents could in truth walk with their heads up-right, for the attorney's failure to appear at the last moment had caused them great harm and grief. And it would have been greater if the failure to appear had not been able to be explained as straightforward as now; for otherwise people would have thought up their own veiled explanations.

Of course people felt sorry for Andijn, but they added: "It was anyways the luck of God that it was prevented – Andijn could thank her God."

***

And now it's Christmas Eve. The air is still and cold, and the sky clear. Large, light gray masses of smoke twist up from the chimneys in the village. Now at dinnertime there is just enough daylight that the Sámi women on the farms around the village can sit and sew without lamplight and it is no colder than that heat from the stove has managed to thaw some oval holes in the ice on the windowpanes.

The village headland is flat with a few ranges of low hills that all go in the same direction toward the riverbank to the west. The small farms are on these hills. In the middle of one of these hills stands the church, a cruciform church of wood. The upper part of the steeple is turnip shaped, probably following Finnish-Russian designs; the church had been built at the beginning of the nineteenth century.

On the highest hill, south of the church, the master smith Jongo has his farm. Olle, a little, pale, black-haired boy, son of the smith, and the hired man are in the yard chopping Christmas wood. There lay large stacks of fresh birch and bare fir. But the minister's and Hooch's and the sheriff's have dry cordwood for the entire year.

Olle takes a quick look at the yard of the big shot, forest ranger and mayor Linde's farmstead on the hill below, right above the church. The woodpile down there threatens to be significantly larger than Olle's and the hired man's, so they really had to keep at it. But Olle had to run over to Erki Lemik Issak's farm that lay on the same hill as the smith's, but closer to the riverbank. Yeah, there they had a large pile already; but then too there were just grown men chopping there; and they needed more wood there, for they had a fireplace in the large room, and a chimney so wide and straight that a reindeer calf from the sky above could fall down through it without getting a spot of soot on it before it was roasted on the coals.

Here in the yard are a few storehouses, the smith's own, the reindeer Sámi Vilge Jouna's storehouse and the reindeer Sámi Andi Lasse's storehouse. Reindeer Sámi families lodge with the Sámi farmers in the winter and have their herds and tents and herders and dogs in the valley areas further up or in the small valleys on the plateaus south of the main valley.

On the village roads can be seen frost-covered horses dragging large timbers and hay and loads of moss and they breathe white rays out of their nostrils.

But already early in the morning bells and sleigh bells had begun to tinkle and blare; entire horse caravans stream down the high, steep wooded hill on the north side of the river. They are folks from the nearest fjord bottom north of the low mountain plateau; it's only 60 miles to there. Most of them are half Kvens; for generations they have gone around in a sort of Sámi costume, but among themselves they only speak *kvensk* (Finnish). They live around the mouth of a short river that runs out into the fjord bottom to the north.

They have probably spent the night at the mountain hostel at Nattvannet. It is an old custom to come up here to the inland village every Christmas, and their only celebration of the year. And they bring along cod-liver oil and dried fish and homespun blankets and gloves, for they trade with the reindeer Sámi here.

Some also come from the east, up the valley, from the small, solitary groups of farms that lie on both sides of the great river that forms the national border down there.

Olle laughs and says:

"Look at that one there! He's riding a burro! (a little steer)."

28

"It's old, poor master Aslak Port, from a small, solitary place far down there. He makes the finest imaginable reindeer sleighs." Olle has heard that master Aslak could be busy with one such sleigh for an entire month. Solid raw material could be found in the birch forest and dried thoroughly, and he uses heartwood of pine for the wide, low 'keel' under the sleigh. And then he rarely got more than ten kroner for such a fine reindeer sled. Had it only been a simple load sled! Olle himself had seen master Aslak sell such a fine sled at his neighbor's, Erki Lemik Issak. Aslak could buck up to insist on 12 kroner; but then he always looked so timid and crushed, and when the buyer said ten, Aslak immediately accepted. And no one was ashamed of bargaining.

Now Aslak has two reindeer sleds on the sleigh. He walks alongside the little, yellowish white steer with the brown flanks. The steer walks with small, stodgy steps, and Aslak every so often gives it a little, encouraging push with his fist in the threadbare reindeer skin glove. He has surely used his three days to cover the 45 miles from Port up to here. Who had seen master Aslak fly through life and this world? Who had seen him pick a fight? No, he was always so calm and silent and had a bit of the fear of life flashing in his small, runny eyes. A really nice log cabin he had down in Port. Ask Our Lord what he and his family lived on! And Our Lord perhaps answers: that is my secret.

♦

But now a bell sound and noisy yoiking are heard that gets everyone to look up.

"*Hoammá!*" the hired man says.

And *hoammá* are the people who live in the Western Plateau parish. Their village is 110 miles from here in a southwesterly direction. And their parish is almost equally large in extent as this one. Erki Lemik Issak, Olle's neighbor, who knows about a little of everything, said that it was three times as big as all of Jarlsberg and Lauravika parishes. The Western Plateau parish lay higher than this one, and the village there was without conifers.

… There are some reindeer Sámi from the border districts of West Plateau parish that come driving; they could already be heard while they were on the ice of the river above the village. They were always grandiose, always came making a racket down to the village here, the harnesses on the draft reindeer resplendent in red and yellow and blue and with shining metal, caps and reindeer coats too. And yoiking at the top of their lungs, they sit half upright, each on his own sled, on one knee, and with the other leg swinging outside the side of the sled. They quickly drive away with the thumb on the rein, yoik and wave their arms, the bells blare. The reindeer drive away in a gallop, in a zigzag, the reindeer sleds swing back and forth. No, they have never learned to drive, these folks. "Our draft reindeer here in the village," the hired man says, "run in a straight line."

But grandiose these people from the Western Plateau district are, and grandiose is their entry wherever they make their entry. Their wives have never learned how to sew reindeer coats and caps and weave belts in a proper Christian way; but everything on them is resplendent in gold and silver and red and blue and yellow. Big blue-eyed bandits to look at are these folks from the western plateau – *o hei o hoi!* and they yoik and holler as if they were full of sweet wine. Some turn into this farm, and some into that one.

***

The church, a cruciform church as said, on Christmas Day is filled by a reindeer coat-clad congregation; but many, especially the younger ones, are in fine, black homespun Sámi costumes with red and yellow and blue borders along the shoulders and on the upright collars. Olle, who is sitting on one of the highest pews, alongside Erki Lemik Issak, can precisely and exactly look at the costumes, and tell where the different people are from. The village people here are of course the best dressed.

Then they sing Christmas hymns in Sámi, and the district curate, a large fat and smooth shaven man with glasses, climbs up into the pulpit; he is in a white mass shirt and speaks in Norwegian. The sexton, who is the interpreter, stands in the choir door.

"Our savior, the Lord Jesus Christ, was born on this night."

"Min beasti, dat Hearrá Jesus Kristus, riegádii dan ija."

Solemn faces are turned first toward the curate in the pulpit and then toward the interpreter in the choir door. So blessed to hear God's word now; it has been a long time, at least as far as the reindeer Sámi are concerned in any case. On the floor in the cloister they all sit who haven't found seats on the pews. And when all is said and done the reindeer Sámi like best to sit with legs crossed on the floor.

There are balconies in each of the three choir rooms connected by narrow walkways around the two protruding corners. And as it were, it was the shabbier, those from the northeastern part of the village, who sought to go there. It was probably a bit gloomy and concealed up there, which inevitably tempted them. Up there sat now for example Batto Andi in a fine, black coat of reindeer calfskin which in no way had been honorably obtained, and with a new psalm book in hand, that he had stolen from the minister's office last fall.

Olle steals a glance behind Erki Lemik Issak's back. Below the lowermost balcony sat the Hoochs and the sheriff's family in a special, closed place for chairs. In a special chair section right by the cross in the middle, sat also the Sámi big shot Linde, "the old sheriff," now mayor and forest ranger. He was a handsome old man, that Linde, like looking at a foreign general.

But Olle's eyes remained stuck on Andijn in the closed section below. On her head with the golden blond hair she had a cap of leather. Such beautiful leather no one had seen before, and Olle didn't know, what sort of animal the hide came from. She had probably gotten that cap on the occasion of her wedding that was supposed to have been now before Christmas … Oh, good God, he must have been insane that man who didn't know how lovely Andijn was! It had been unbelievably beautiful to hear Andijn sing hymns today; and now Olle understood that it somehow wasn't songs the others sang, just screaming and noise. And why was it that Andijn only today should sing more beautifully than ever. Everyone in the church had turned their faces toward her, no, Olle did not understand why they did not remain silent out of pure shame. … Now there was the sermon: but Olle thought he could see on Andijn that she wasn't listening. She sat and looked steadily out through the windows on the north side. Constantly, constantly she sat and looked out through the window even though she could hardly see anything but the sky – the window was too high for that. But Olle didn't know that Andijn sat and listened. Now, during the high mass on Christmas Day no one was out driving … but Andijn sat and listened. It might be that she thought she heard the distant sound of sleigh bells … but maybe it was just whistling in her own ears.

… But there! In the Lord's sanctuary on this first Christmas Day sat also Ågall from the fjord to the north. The sorcerer, the wise and good one, and who didn't just read in the black book, but also in the Holy Writ. Olle croaked! Just this past fall it happened that an evil, a very unjust person, had met ghosts, sent out by Ågall – because the bad man did not want to make good again, what he had committed against his neighbor. Ågall had a somewhat gloomy but otherwise very handsome owl face. His beard reminded one of the feathers on the night bird, and his eyes were round and overpoweringly strong. But no one had yet heard that this man had done anything evil against good peopl; and if he sent out ghosts during the night, he didn't do it for the sake of simple gain.

And otherwise no one was surprised that Ågall, who had come up here with other fjord people, was now sitting in God's holy house. Last Christmas Ågall had been visiting Olle's father, the master smith, and the two men had sat and talked a lot about holy things; and when several others had arrived, Ågall held a little prayer meeting. But Ågall never appeared in meeting places. From what sort of people he came and where he had his lineage no one knew for certain. He appeared as a Sámi among Sámi, as a Norwegian among Norwegians: but one would most probably say that his wife was Sámi. And his entire family out by the fjord had long ago gone over to living in the Sámi way. But Ågall himself could well have been related to people in the land of the Egyptians where Goshen was.

Jørgensen the sheriff's deputy sat too in Hooch's and the sheriff's chair section below, behind Andijn and her parents, even though the Hoochs in a way couldn't stand him; but Jørgensen the sheriff's deputy was a nephew of the sheriff; he was a big, bowlegged giant with a black beard. The tip of the otherwise proper nose was the most remarkable nose tip Our Lord had put on a person; it moved, cut inward with every word he said. People from the sea district said that the nose tip was like a claw on a crab; it moved like a claw joint. He was inordinately clever and greedy. And he did what was almost unknown among proper people up here: he made indecent approaches to married women too. And it wasn't long ago since Olle with his own eyes had seen that he had poked a pregnant widow of a recently deceased reindeer Sámi whose property was up for auction because of unpaid taxes; he had poked her because she had lain weeping over her beloved possessions.

Who is he sitting and gaping at, this Jørgensen the sheriff's deputy? The chair section down there near the door is on the men's side – there is someone on the women's side Jørgensen the sheriff's deputy is sitting and gaping at. It is a young girl. Olle doesn't recognize her, but judging from her attire she must certainly be from the fjord below. Though she is sitting, Olle can see that she must be very tall, as tall as Andijn – and that she resembles Andijn! And she is pretty too, but naturally not as pretty as Andijn, somewhat coarser in the face; no, it is quite impossible to be as pretty and good as Andijn. But there are also others looking at this Sámi girl. The women who are sitting in front almost twist their necks out of joint to catch a glance at her. And now Olle guesses that she must be the daughter of Ågall! So that's it! Jørgensen the sheriff's deputy's eyes were popping out of his head. Involuntarily Andijn suspects, though she is sitting up front, that he is sitting and staring hard at the unfamiliar girl over on the women's side; she turns her head a bit – yes, quite right. And it was as if Andijn's wandering thoughts at this moment took another direction ... The more present occupied them, although Jørgensen the sheriff's deputy was not alone indifferent to her, but simply disgusting, had always been. But now he sat here and stared at the girl over on the women's side.

⋅

The district curate said amen, and then there was hymn singing again. It could have been so glorious if Andijn's beautifully sounding song down below hadn't laid bare the others' unaesthetic screeching.

While the people were streaming out of the church, a man had an attack out on the steps; he staggered, and his distorted face was frightful to look at. Two merciful men took and carried him out and laid him down on the snow. People were certain that – and Olle also heard someone hint at it aloud – well, that evil spirits had been awaiting the man out on the steps, since such spirits dare not come into the sanctuary itself. The two men who had carried him out each borrowed a Sámi knife from a couple of reindeer Sámi from the West Plateau district; they were the only folks wearing belted knives in the church, and they put the knives up under the armpits of the possessed; for that kind of spirit gladly yields to steel.

"So, he has epilepsy, the poor thing, says Ågall."

"Epilepsy?" A man said in an angry tone; it was as if he wanted to uphold the evil spirits' honor. "You shouldn't speak so loud about epilepsy in this case, you, Ågall."

And others thought it was bold of the man to speak in such a tone to Ågall!

The red-bearded sheriff stood and read announcements from the church-yard, while his wife, a beautiful, competent person went over to the unfamiliar slender Sámi girl she had seen in the church, and whom she thought she had to say hello to. Yes, the girl was the daughter of Ågall and her name was Anga. And right away Jørgensen the sheriff's deputy was there; the tip of his nose cut inward, like a crab claw joint, as if it had gotten epilepsy too. Now Andijn too would gladly like to have greeted the unfamiliar girl; she felt an involuntary need to get to know her, be on intimate terms with her, somehow get her under her own care. But now she didn't want to get mixed up in it.

⋅

Anda Piera, Per Andersen, the delightfully flippant and so remarkable Norwegian to look at, he too, stood up proudly on the steps of his little, old, tumbledown house on the church hill, right in front of the church, and entertained his audience. He shared the house with his brother Juoksa and his two sisters Inga and Marit. None of them were married, and with the exception of Juoksa they were already quite old. The sisters had had such large noses, and such long, narrow faces – no, they weren't passable women in these parts. But for Juoksa, the youngest, there will be hope for a long time in the future, and he had daring talent; for although the four siblings belong to and were related to the respectable, southern part of the village, Juoksa could sometimes surprise the others so that one morning a reindeer carcass lay in the storehouse.

And such order there was in this house! Not a stick of wood was out of place in the yard or by the fireplace, not a herring was wasted in this house. They each had their own locked chest under each one's bed in the living room, and each their own housekeeping. So they sat there each on the edge of their beds and spoke the most correct Sámi traditional language imaginable.

Anda Piera, the second oldest of the four, stood on the steps as said and entertained some church folks; he had a large, bent nose, a huge row of teeth and short-clipped beard. He always held his little old tobacco pipe between his lips with his hand and not between his teeth in order to spare the mouthpiece. There was again talk of horses, and Anda Piera says to Erki Lemik Issak, a well-to-do man with quite a few possessions, and who recently had bought a large, black stallion from Finland:

"Although my horse is 12 years old I am nevertheless ready to race with you at any time."

Now Barjo Sammul also stood here, a reindeer Sámi. He says:

"And I challenge you, Anda Piera, to race with me. I'll take my wife's draft reindeer. And then we'll see whether I will have to look back in order to see what became of you and your mare."

Anda Piera laughed and said to poor master Aslak from Port who was also standing here, silent and sort of with a bit of fear for his life:

"You, master Aslak, you who have such a fast burro, can't you challenge Burjo Sammul to a race?"

People laughed; Burjo Sammul got angry and said:

"I haven't seen your riverboat, Anda Piera, since we reindeer Sámi are not here in the inland during the summer. But I have heard that that boat is supposed to be over 30 years old, in other words more than twice as old as your stallion, and of the old *Goski-gjerdi* type that you can't get anywhere with on a river. And you have never seen a boat of the new *Jongo-gjerdi* type that the master smith himself has made, and that somehow goes by itself up all the rapids. Others have had a dozen boats during the time you have puttered around with the old one. And a new horse you won't get either as long as the old one can walk stiffly out of the stall."

Anda Piera rose up proudly and was greedily provoked:

"If you dare race, Burjo Sammul, then so do I!"

"So race, damn it!" someone shouted, and the churchgoers who hadn't yet gone home were all enthusiastic.

Burjo Sammul went to the woods, to the hillside on the north to get his reindeer; when the reindeer Sámi who had come down here to the village just to spend several days at Christmas, they usually had their draft reindeer in the hillsides down here during that period.

There was racing down on the ice of the river. Anda Piera sat and lifted his head up in the sleigh and was like Kaiser Wilhelm to look at where he sat riding with tight reins, and the gray gelding lifted his head and ran away like a sun-happy hare during the color change. And Anda Piera won. He wasn't consumed with the victory, but how he rose proudly! And with this began a new era in the little, old cottage on the church hill. Burjo Sammul never completely recovered after this defeat; in any case the need for display had sort of ebbed out.

***

During the evening of Christmas Day Hooch had a magnificent display of fireworks in the yard, the first people here had seen of this kind of fire.

But during Christmas afternoon it was as if the sleigh bells began getting busy, from the southernmost district in the village and all the way down to the gloomy district to the northeast. The harness in the hallway was taken down from the peg. It rang carefully, and young girls who were sitting in the living room got sort of a world of music through themselves. The harness was carried out into the yard; some of the girls and other young people standing in the yard or sitting on the storehouse steps gave a start; the horse in the stall heard it best and pricked his ears. The horse doesn't normally have sleigh bells.

A large, Finnish-Russian sleigh is pulled out. The rowboat-like, loose elegant box is scraped of ice and moss and hay and lashed to the sleigh.

Halle Johanas, a slender, blond Sámi farmer, a very handsome young man, is getting himself ready. He is going to drive, and drive with Andijn. She herself had asked him about it already before Christmas. Halle Johanas is son of one of the two farms highest up. He wears an elegant fur coat of the finest reindeer calf skin, black and shorthaired; it falls into folds like silk. With such an elegant coat no belt is worn. The upright collar that goes over the chest opening in a bow has a border of scarlet cloth, continuing as two loops down the chest. And inside is the collar.

Many wanted to be friends with Halle Johanas. He had snow white, straight Sámi shoes, and leggings of the shiny kind, shorthaired skin, that was lengthened with scarlet cloth around the ankle, tied around the leg on the snow white Sámi shoes.

It was a large, red-haired mare he harnessed up. The high wooden yoke held the shafts tight so the horse had more room and the hames didn't lean backwards. Up on the wooden collar were the large sleigh bells.

Who Halle Johanas would take along was known, but there were many a young swain who kept it secret. One came driving and stopped on the road below the big shot Linde; here there were several girls in the yard, full of excitement. The one who stopped walked with firm steps into the small side room and came out with Marja. Others captured their girl at other farmyards; some girls put up a little resistance. A couple of reindeer Sámi girls were much sought after this Christmas; they had fine silk frocks and silver and gold rings.

Halle Johanas could really and truly drive down the village, over the church hill, past the sheriff's farmyard, past the parsonage; and really and truly stop in the yard outside Hooch's large house. Here there was nothing to hide, nothing to divine. Andijn was young and had to go out driving. And whom else should she choose other than Halle Johanas. He was certainly more than a coach boy, even for a girl like Andijn. He was a bit of a cavalier.

Marvelous how Andijn had been able to take it with composure, this depressing incident before Christmas. And now on Christmas Day she had blessed all the people with the most beautiful hymn singing that had yet been heard under this church's vault. And today the Hoochs had as usual had guests for dinner, and besides the sheriff's family and the district curate, the Sámi big shot, mayor and forest ranger Linde along with the master smith Jongo had been there. It was an old custom that the two good Sámi should be guests however great and fine a feast it might be. And now little Olle, the master smith's son, had also been invited to come and eat apples. So Olle was present and could delight in Andijn's stepping up into the sleigh of Halle Johanas. The guests had all been very much in agreement that it was better for Andijn to get out instead of sitting inside and entertaining them.

Oh, how Halle Johanas' red mare could start off! At speed past the sheriff's farm, Andijn caught a glimpse of Jørgensen the sheriff's deputy and the sorcerer Ågall's daughter: they were going out driving with Erki Lemik Issak's young, black stallion. So, wasn't it what Andijn had feared? Since yesterday when she had become aware of Anga, Ågall's daughter, in the church, she had had an unpleasant notion that Anga would get into Jørgensen's claws. And if it hadn't been that people would just easily misunderstand, then she would have undertaken that sacrifice and committed to a driving trip with Jørgensen, just to frustrate Anga's falling into his claws.

And now she had an idea that lifted her inner vision: she would meet Ågall, Anga's father, before he traveled down to the fjord again. Not only on the occasion of this with Anga and Jørgensen: she wanted to consult him about what concerned herself and about Einar Asper. No, she wouldn't get Ågall to inflict some harm on Einar, but raise the veil a little. Andijn got passionate at the thought of this. And all sorts of visions popped up for her, the space became freer, larger.

◆

The entire village resounded and blared from sleigh bells enthroned on the high wooden collar and from large bells tied fast to the shafts diagonally so they rang better, and from small bell rings below the belly of the horse.

No, it wasn't a sleigh ride, as such. Everyone drove his own way. Some stopped at a farm yard and poured out of a silver beaker; the horses were sweaty and in trotter form. Others drove outside the village. Halle Johanas and Andijn drove down onto the ice on the river above the village, and as they rounded the point of the headland over on the other side, Halle Johanas began to yoik a new melody. For him it was the past that first sang out a new melody; the other youths then took and added the small, rambling words. They always sing out to particular persons, and it is the person concerned who in a way determines the melody's character and tone.

Andijn sat and listened; she knew all the yoik melodies here, but not this one. So beautifully and warmly only Halle Johanas could yoik. He proceeded tentatively, was silent a bit, and again went on. They had come all the way up to the next headland point, and then Halle Johanas sang it out. Andijn grasped him by the arm.

"You created that now, Johanas?"

"Yes."

No, Andijn didn't want to ask him about more; she let him yoik. And now it again became alive for her the evening before Christmas. She had stood on the riverbank in the village and listened and listened, and then she took to walking down on the ice of the river and staring down where the winter road turned from the headland down and out onto the ice. She had looked at the reflection of light on the road, that it was northern lights, the airy, fluttering, silky thin blankets of fire right up there under the sky and all of its stars … when she had walked and listened for a sleigh bell sound, in vain, so the sky above her had almost darkened anyway.

That wasn't so long ago; but much of it had sort of already transformed itself. And had been emancipated, and had gotten a milder light over it. So that's how it was when someone had suffered, had had to struggle; to be sure it was fruitless to struggle and then struggle more. The next week the mail came from the east, and then she would hear what had become of Einar. Einar Asper … Care for him? No, now it was as if her heart didn't want to have confidence that she would care for him. And at some moments the whole thing could appear like a distant, bad dream to her.

◆

Andijn had a little silver lark inside her reindeer coat; Halle Johanas stopped the horse.

Then they turned around, and the big, frisky, red mare started to trot by itself.

"Sing more – the same," Andijn said.

And when they had swung up onto the village headland again Andijn also sang along, in a new, enchanted joy. She knew the melody, her own. And although the village was full of bell sounds Andijn's and Halle Johanas' beautiful, high voices could be heard at a long distance; people pricked their ears – what was it? And the other melody masters could sort of hear that it was a melody about Andijn. About Andijn that evening before Christmas. Even the large, red mare seemed to get its fiery joy from the song, and the bells. It raised its head as if listening up into the air. Everyone that stood in the different farmyards or stood in the passages knew and heard well that it was Andijn and Halle Johanas. And now all the people on these Christmas days had heard in the church how Andijn's hymn singing had been full of a great jubilation and praising of God. But now? No, it could not be denied that this was a heathen song, and the beauty in it, when you come right down to it, could not make amends for it.

◆

They drove over the church hill; they didn't stop outside Hooch, for Andijn didn't want to. They just continued further down the village, down onto the ice on the river below, where Andijn that evening before Christmas had walked alone and had been afraid of hearing loud sighs coming from her own chest … Now she wanted to sing and exorcise that evening's shadows, melt away the clump that had sat in her chest and was still sitting there. But, here it failed for Andijn, she couldn't bring forth her voice, nor Halle Johanas either. They hurried to turn around, had become somehow so silent and withdrawn.

… No, Andijn didn't want to go home again, for now her voice and song came forth again, of its own accord. People who were standing on the church hill could see in the strong northern lights and moonlight that the large, red mare had flakes of froth on its sides; but it seemed to hurry forth without its hooves touching the ice.

+

Elle, citizen Sire Andaras' daughter, stood leaning against the entryway outside Erki Lemik Issak's house, together with some other youths. There stood Mikkal too, and as a reindeer Sámi he didn't have any rides with horses to offer. Besides he felt miserable after a binge and a fight he had come upon yesterday evening.

Elle stood half hidden behind the other girls; well, she had first decided to hide herself completely. She didn't want … if he came …

Olle was also here – to keep an eye on Elle – if Mikkal wanted to take and lead her up to the attic!

Suddenly Andi Piera's sleigh bells are heard; the big, black stallion comes at full trot and swings into the farmyard here. Andi Piera jumps up from the sleigh and wants to go in, discovers Elle in the throng and grabs her. Elle thinks about resisting a little, but lets herself be led to the sleigh anyway. And off it went.

It heads up through the village and down onto the ice on the river … But Elle bitterly succumbs to her sorrow that she let herself be captured. Mikkal remained standing there so wretched and dispirited. Elle breaks into tears.

They had reached the point on the upper headland when the speed stopped. Andi Piera pulled a bottle up from his reindeer coat, poured into a silver goblet and handed it to Elle. No, Elle didn't want to take it.

"Shouldn't we turn back again?" she says.

But then they hear a lovely, yoiking woman's voice. It is just Andijn, Hooch's daughter, *Hooká nieida*, who had such a voice; and they recognized it. But she yoiked so wild and enchantingly! They had probably heard her sing and yoik before too, but never such as now.

On the way home Andi Piera tried to take hold of Elle's hand; but she kept her arms folded over her chest, with the hands stuck each in the opposite sleeve.

The sleigh ride spreads out over the village, and people standing in the farmyards by the common roads each said, on their own side:

"Look, there is Andi Piera with Elle in the sleigh; yeah, that's quite a pair! And there is Halle Johanas with *Hooká nieida* in the sleigh!" And people laughed: "yeah, that Halle Johanas! always together with higher-ups!"

The sleigh bells continued to boom resoundingly throughout the village until far into the evening. The good trotters ran with long strides, steaming and wringing wet, with frost flakes here and there; and they had been so excited by the speed that a little blow with a whip now felt just like encouragement. Suddenly Halle Johanas' horse toppled over just when it was going to go up a hill and past Ville Jongo's farm. People came running and looked at the poor animal with horror; blood and foam gushed out of the nostrils. Ville Jongo came too, and he said to Halle Johanas, during the others' grave silence:

"People who drink themselves drunk on a holiday in this manner can do the outrageous and revolting as you have done here, Halle Johanas. There lies your horse as a result of brutal riding."

Andijn then said to Ville Jongo:

"Yes, it is outrageous and revolting, and it is my fault. Halle Johanas has not been drunk. It was I, who steadily asked him to drive fast and without stop. But now I understand what I have done."

No, you probably couldn't have helped it, poor thing, thought Ville Jongo, but he didn't say it.

+

After the sleigh ride the young swains each went with his girl to his own room to lie and chat on the bed – in all reasonable propriety. Andi Piera who was afraid that Elle would rush away got his old father to unhitch the horse and take care of it. And now he dragged Elle with force into the room. There were a few standing in the farmyard, and out of common decency it wasn't possible for Elle to get away from him without having been in his room. But Elle refused to let him feel her up under the coat and costume.

+

The dead horse was taken home to Halle Johanas. Andijn followed along.

"You must come home with me, Johanas, so that we can explain it to my parents, and I want them to see that you are not drunk."

… Halle Johanas went home with her.

… Andijn followed him to the doorway when he had said goodbye to *Hooká* and his wife. She stood so close to him that Johanas got dizzy. Then he said goodbye also to her; on the way home he opened his eyes, and he still thought he smelled her and her spirit; but the horse had fallen dead – and the other thing could be a mistake. Halle Johanas was so cheerful and young.

But *Hooká* had not mentioned anything to him about wanting to give Halle Johanas compensation for the horse.

Gumppet ja Bohccot
Wolves and Reindeer

Right after New Year's the long distance traveling Christmas guests began to go to their districts. Some herders from the fjord just to the north had held a stormy meeting in Anna Johanar's fine residence; but none of the village's own had yet been carried along. Those from the sea district had bartered for reindeer sinew to sew with, reindeer blood in reindeer stomachs, skin from the skin on the reindeer shanks that is used for the finer Sámi shoes and skins of the lower legs, pants legs; and the few who could afford it had bought whole reindeer carcasses. And the reindeer Sámi had in return gotten large, thick woolen blankets for winter tents, fermented cod-liver oil in sheep stomachs for processing and greasing skins with, and homespun cloth, for pants and jackets; women's clothing was colored with pot black.

◆

It hadn't been possible for Elle, citizen Sire Andaras' daughter, to speak with Mikkal alone these days, and she couldn't well reproach him for it either, after what had happened Christmas Day when she had let herself be taken up into the sleigh of Andi Piera, and Mikkal just stood there, so wretched and abandoned.

The third day of the new year she learned that Mikkal intended to travel up to his *siida* the next day, his reindeer camp; it was in the western valley district way up – citizen Sire Andaras' *siida* was in the southern. The valleys met about ten miles above the village, just above the Sámi farmers' summer pastures. And Elle says to her father:

"Now it's time that we travel up to our *siida*. We cannot let Gonge and old *hoammá* Aslak be there alone now, when word is about that there are wolves in the Enare district in Finland. Mother of course will stay here; but you and I have to go."

And her father was in agreement. But now her father said to her:

"You were out driving with Andi Piera Christmas Day – and I know he is in love with you. Mother and I would like you to marry a farmer's son, and we can't think of a better man for you than Andi Piera, the only bachelor here who owns both horse and house and other property even though he is not married."

Elle turned away and uttered moodily that there were other bachelors who were just as good as Andi Piera.

It was still dark when towards morning Sire Andaras went on skis up to the wooded slope on the south side of the village to find the draft reindeer that now for the holiday and together with other good folks' draft reindeer had run loose in the pastures up on the grassy hillside.

◆

In the late afternoon Elle and her father were hitching the reindeer to the sleds in the farmyard of Erki Lemik Issak. Then they heard the bell sound and a boisterous yoiking. It was Mikkal who came driving at full speed up the village's main road; oh, how his magnificent voice sounded during this wild ride!

Sire Andaras suddenly found that first he had to go in *Hooká's* country store; but Elle said they had along everything they needed to have – her countenance was so grumpy and defiant – and thereby she drove off. Sire Andaras found it best not to go to the country store that was further down on the lower river-bank, and he drove away too.

Sire Andaras had driven onto the ice around the first river headland above the village when he heard the sound of sleigh bells. He looked back, and it was Andi Piera's big, black stallion that came trotting up at full speed. Sire Andaras slowed down.

Yes, Andi Piera wanted to ask whether he could be allowed to make a *soagŋu* trip, courting journey, to Elle this winter. Sire Andaras was moved and asked him by all means to come.

But he immediately had to hurry on so as not to lose sight of Elle.

But Elle let her white reindeer travel, and about that reindeer people said it was as if it sailed. It was in vain for her father to try to catch up to her. At the point of every river headland she was on the watch for a glimpse of Mikkal who was ahead; but Mikkal too had a reindeer that sailed.

Elle stopped first above the Sámi farmers' summer pastures, where the valley divides into two. Mikkal had disappeared up into the valley district that went toward the southwest – Elle and her father were going up the one that went to the south.

Elle sat and looked up the valley to the southwest. No, poor Mikkal didn't know that a little girl was riding after him and trying to catch up to him, or was it just because he knew that he wasn't going to let himself be caught. Elle let her white reindeer eat snow and dig for moss at the edge of the woods. Her father arrived: but they didn't exchange many words, and not a word about what they both had at heart. Then they drove further up their own valley. Three miles further lay a solitary farm, the only one up here. They stopped there and told the news from the village while they ate and drank coffee. It was already entirely dark.

Here the sleigh road ended; now there was just a crooked sled road that led further up – in part over the ice, in part through willow and birch scrub in those places where the rapids in the river had made the ice impassable.

It was already rather late in the evening when a few miles farther up they swung into a side road to the west side that led up to a wooded slope.

The dogs, who of course owned the whole thing, both tent and the people and the herd, came down shrieking, but seemed literally to have been struck dumb when they discovered that it was the master of the household and Elle. They were barely able to give off a few small, whimpering howls of joy where they ran along the sleds – soon they greeted Elle and soon Sire Andaras.

Gonge, the servant, and *hoammá* Aslak ambled out of the servants' tent when they heard the dogs sing up. *Hoammá* Aslak was in a way lodging with Sire Andaras; he didn't have more than seventy, eighty reindeer, and it was nothing to have his own *siida* with, and besides he was an old bachelor.

Hoammá Aslak said to Gonge:

"Wonder whether he has *jugástat* – a nip – to offer us."

They got a fire kindled in the master of the household's tent, and the kettle that hung over the fireplace in the middle of the tent got cooking. The master of the household's draft reindeer had been let loose, and they had immediately headed to the woods in the direction where the herd could be smelled; but the aroma of reindeer moss was too tempting for them to continue on. And they actually dived under the snow with the front of their bodies, stretched forward so the snow sprayed around the powerful antlers, and with their muzzles and the front teeth in the lower jaw – the reindeer doesn't have teeth in the upper jaw – loosened the reindeer moss and stuck their heads up from the snow and chewed.

✦

47

Sire Andaras sat on his reindeer hide over a layer of brush that went around the tent and looked somewhat moody, didn't say much, only asked whether there was peace.

"No, we have not noticed wolves at all," says Gonge, "but, he said, a reindeer disappeared, one of those the Sámi recognize among a thousand."

"Then that damned David Piera has been out again," Sire Andaras says.

"I think rather it was one of the Sámi farmers who has been up here for the holidays."

They had eaten, and now Elle pulled a bottle out of the sealskin bag.

"*Nuvi Ipmil!* Oh, God. Did you really bring along *jugástat* with you, Elle!" says Gonge – and *hoammá* Aslak actually smiled sincerely. Sire Andaras too had to smile: for it was precisely liquor he had thought of buying when they were going to drive from the village when Elle drove from him, not because he himself cares about liquor; but something like that he had to have along.

Gonge who hadn't tasted strong or nearly pure alcohol since last year – he hadn't yet been down in the village this winter – held his throat open in the most hospitable way, while he held the bottle to his mouth. In silence he handed the bottle to Sire Andaras; in silence Sire Andaras handed it to *hoammá* Aslak, and it was with a serious expression in his five-sided face the latter let the bottle do full justice.

"*Gittos eatnat*, mange takk!"

"Yeah, *gittos eatnat!*"

And they sat quiet and serious for a while, and then another round came. And again a little silent time.

Gonge was an unkempt giant in a threadbare reindeer coat; his hair hung over the coat collar, and his big, protruding blue eyes were a little sore from smoke. But now it was calm weather and the smoke went nicely up through the smoke vent.

"Yeah, one more *jugástat*," said Sire Andaras, and *hoammá* Aslak's thin, flat face blushed; he pulled his legs in under the seat – he had to do something at this moment – and he also patted himself on the mouth, sort of in advance. Then there was talk about everything that had happened in the village and in the wider world. There hadn't been a court session this fall, but there would be one in March, and then there would also be the district governor and the bishop; and the district governor will naturally have gold clothing on when he holds a meeting in the courtroom. And the bailiff will judge reindeer thieves and other thieves; but attorney Jakobsen knows his law, he too; he is supposed to be just as good in the law as the district governor – although he drinks, and it's too bad, for he could have been district governor.

Elle pulled a nice bread up from the sealskin bag and a large birch bark box with butter in it, the box Sire Andaras had bought from a Russian skipper from Archangel.

"And you have cow butter with you too! Yes, you Elle, nice bread! It'll be like a wedding here!"

In the innermost spot in the tent were pots and cups and tubs of leather and birch burls, and coffee and sugar bags and such. And there was also a chest, an oval trunk of curved birch, and it had an arched cover and brass fittings. The cover wall was also of curved birch, joined with a pleated cut into the main wall and in the leaf end, and it looked as if both were made of the same birch board. It was a family heirloom made by Sire Andaras' grandfather; that he had worked an entire year on it wasn't too much.

Elle laughs and says:

"You know what people have begun to call father now? … He's called nothing other than *boargár*, citizen, Sire Andaras now."

"*Boargár*! – *boargár* Sire Andaras! Who in the hell came up with that!" Gonge laughs.

"Yes, Erki Lemik Issak did," and now Sire Andaras himself laughed too – the nickname had flattered him as well.

♦

The next day it was also nice and calm weather, and at noontime there was good daylight too; but the sun wouldn't come up before the 21st of January. The snow on the wooded slopes around here had been tramped down in a circumference miles wide; the herd grazed very spread out on these peaceful slopes when there were no wolves to be noticed. Reindeer coats and homespun pants and reindeer meat were hanging on the tree branches, and a few sleds stood raised up against the pine trunks.

Gonge and Sire Andaras had made a round on the slope early in the morning to look after the herd, and here there could well be about a thousand reindeer, all Sire Andaras', with the exception of the seventy-eighty that belonged to his lodger, *hoammá* Aslak, and the thirty that belonged to *reaŋga*, the hired man, Gonge.

Now Gonge and *hoammá* Aslak stood and marveled at the fine, new driving sled of Elle that Sire Andaras had bought from master Aslak at Christmas. They turned it around and considered it from all sides and ran their fingers over it. The heartwood in the wide, flat keel was like polished steel. They raised the sled up to see whether they could find a little light between the board joints.

"Not enough to stick a hair through," says Gonge.

The fine, narrow and, on the outside, arched boards of birch, seven on each side of the keel, were one by one joined together along a thin, diagonally attached edge; and one by one attached with wooden pegs to some thin ribs of curved birch. In front they bent and twisted, narrowing together into a high, fine slope, and the thin pieces were joined into the stretched-out, high prow and squeezed in with a thin, double shank sinew that was pulled through a couple holes and fastened with wooden pegs. And then the round, arched back support!

Not a spike, not an iron nail. But first and foremost it was the beautiful, beautiful lines in this driving sled that got Gonge's eyes to rest desirously on it.

***

A couple weeks had passed, and Sire Andaras waited now for Andi Piera to come with escort as suitor. He would have preferred that it should happen in the village under great pomp and circumstance, and with the whole village as spectators. But Elle didn't want to go down to the village now, by any means.

One night of moonlight it was so quiet here on the wooded slope; everyone slept peacefully, the dogs too. But the old dog Girjes, the motley colored one who was missing one forepaw – he had once stepped onto a set fox trap – no, Girjes didn't find it reasonable that everyone slept at one time. He lay up against the master and watched and listened – you never know. A little, distant sigh – what? And Girjes jumped up, but without barking, pushed with his snout the distended blanket door up and slipped out. Girjes listened, still without barking. Then he heard a couple of bad, bad howls. Girjes let out a howl, so that he was on the verge of losing his voice. The dogs in the tent came wandering out, sleep drunk and baying. Girjes went in and made a big racket, and in the next instant the people and dogs were at full speed up the wooded slope, branches cracked as if it was angry steers on the move.

The herd rushed around spread like rags in a whirlwind; the dogs bayed in a horrible earnestness. Girjes and another dog had directed their attack against a wolf following Elle's white draft reindeer. The reindeer rushed in wild leaps over snowdrifts and small bushes; but the wolf was catching up with it more and more. Girjes who was lacking a forepaw knew himself that it was in vain to carry out a direct pursuit. He had chosen the tactic of being careful to be where he presumed the wolf would come rushing; and it was as if the white reindeer also understood this tactic, or whether it was because it involuntarily sought rescue with Girjes — in any case, the cooperation was there. The other dog, large and long-legged, black and somewhat shorthaired, was after the wolf the entire time, close on its heels. Now this wild retinue, whose lungs at the same time were plagued with fear and blood thirst and blind hatred of the enemy, came down a slope and right toward Girjes. And hardly had the wolf abruptly turned against the snapping, large dog behind itself, before Girjes had sunk his old, but still solid teeth into the testicles of the wolf that now suddenly let out a yell that seemed to come from hell. But Girjes didn't let go, and what weakened him now was that the wolf managed to bite him a couple times; die he would gladly do, but let go, never! The big dog understood the situation immediately, and it occupied the wolf from another angle, and Girjes could do entirely as he wished and take the wolf's life. He bit his teeth farther and farther in, snarled deeply and shaking now and then through the nostrils — as if to incite his own bloodshot savagery; he was positively in another world at this instant, full of a victorious joy at being able to press the life out of an enemy — the complete battle display let loose — yet one more time able to be the completely wild animal.

◆

This was late in January, and the sun had already shown itself on the horizon to the south.

The people and the dogs strove day and night to gather the herd that was now spread in all directions. As far as one can understand there were probably not more than 3-5 wolves that had been active — and it was probably some of the wolves that according to rumors had harried in the Enare districts of Finland, so approximately 150 miles from here. And these wolves from the east, they have often come wandering all the way from the Russian tundra to the north when famine and hunger drove them westward. To begin with, they could have been up to a hundred together; they have attacked reindeer herds on the way, been chased away; some have eaten themselves to death on poison bait; others have fallen to a lead bullet from an old flintlock. Some have been surprised just as they have eaten themselves half to death on a reindeer, have taken to foot and thrown up willingly so as to be able to flee more easily. Damn beasts, they have become cunning and shrewd from inherited and their own experiences of predatory behavior. Even if ever so hungry, they travel around first in large rings to ascertain whether there might be some of the dangerous two-legged animals nearby; not a sound do they emit when they are out on such a reconnaissance trip. But if they are alone, and no prey is to be glimpsed, see, then it is heard, the howl like unholy wilderness; and then it happens to be sure that they choose a victim among their own – life shall be saved, even of the accursed! Undoubtedly for no other reason than that it is life.

+

One of the 3-4 wolves had fallen to Girjes' teeth – and Girjes continued to be a wild animal for many days. A couple of reindeer bitten to death were found further down in the valley – on one of them the entrails had been ripped out – the beasts of prey want to get hold of the fat kidneys and such. But the other 2-3 wolves had managed to flee – none of the people had seen them; but the dogs had probably been aggressive enough, and the wildly shouting human voices had been too unpleasant for the wolves to have dared to go on eating for very long. Their tracks led over the low plateau between this valley and the valley farther west – where Mikkal and his parents and siblings were staying this winter.

Elle had thought it might be right and proper that Gonge go over the plateau to warn them over there in the other valley; but the others didn't want to listen – hardly for any other reason than that you didn't usually sacrifice yourself so much for others' welfare. Besides, Sire Andaras eagerly wanted to have taken a trip there; but he had his own reason for that: had any of his own reindeer come there, after the wolves had scattered the herd, then Mikkal could probably have hit on slaughtering some of them; and it would have done Elle good to discover, see for herself that Mikkal was that way, rich man's son, but a thief. And it was rather not for nothing that he was from the West Plateau district; even Mikkal's costume still reminded of that – even though he was only a child when they came moving from there.

All of eight days had passed, and still three hundred reindeer were missing, and *hoammá* Aslak cried over the loss of three of his own. Word got about that the wolves had ravaged the herd, also in other districts, and the reindeer Sámi had been down in the village to get poison. A couple hunters went to the place where the wolf had ravaged; and about one of them, the old Anti Lemik, it was said that he usually wet his eyes with tobacco oil to sharpen his sight when he was going to shoot.

The reindeer Sámi were now busy making trips to each other's tents in the valleys and on the plateaus to look for lost reindeer – and found one or more. For in this district, three times larger than Jarlsberga and Lauravika counties, the people from the heights were generally quite honorable.

But this district's people had little by little become poor. It came in part from the custom they had had from old: when in the spring they had come up to *Spierttanjárga*, one of the large, long peninsulas to the northeast, they left their herds untended, and they themselves began to sleep the whole spring and summer to its end along the sea coast. Good for the reindeer in that respect, as they got to roam freely on the peninsula's large, moss-rich plateaus. The cows were not milked, so the milk benefited the calves. But in the fall when the reindeer on their own took to moving to the interior toward the large inland valley again, then the Sámi had to follow along for weeks and months in the autumn sleet and all kinds of weather, round up and separate, little by little as they advanced. And there were stretches of 120-150 miles. And when they sometime in October or November had finally come to the winter pastures in the inland tracts again, then there were often numerous reindeer missing. Already at the end of August the meat kettles were bubbling in the resident reindeer thieves' homes in the inland valley. Entirely openly these shady rogues boasted of their well being; and although not once did they buy reindeer in an honorable way, they had reindeer meat hanging up for drying in the spring like other well-off Sámi farmers.

Yes, it had gone very much downhill in this district for the people from the heights.

But Sire Andaras and a couple of others had begun the practice of going up to the *Gáisá* glacier on the peninsula just to the north with Nordkapp-Magerøy beyond. There they tended the herd all spring, summer and fall, milked the cows and had cheese and frozen reindeer milk in the reindeer stomachs during the fall. And it was some 90-120 miles up to the *Gáisá* glaciers and the pastures to the north.

◆

So it happened one night, a few days after the wolf night, that while Sire Andaras and Elle and the dogs lay sleeping, a large, flapping creature came falling down through the smoke hole. The dogs jumped up terrified and barking – Elle and Sire Andaras leapt up – the creature flapped and flew around like a bewildered spook from the realm of the dead; the dogs howled and didn't dare attack – and finally the monster tumbled up and through the smoke hole again. It was an eagle owl, and heaven knows what it wanted here; perhaps the dark space had seemed enticing to its darkness loving soul.

Both Elle and Sire Andaras were so shaken that they could hardly speak; and for a while after they heard the eagle owl's melancholy *hu-hu* from the wooded hillside. They stoked up the fire in the hearth, and they discovered that old Girjes lay there stone dead. The wolf night had taken it out on his old heart, and he hadn't tolerated this frightful shock now. Had a new wolf surprised him in the tent, Girjes would probably have been man enough to refrain from losing his wits and mind. But this unknown that came flapping down through the smoke hole at this moment was too much for Girjes.

+

One day a man stopped in the yard outside the tents; he had three, four reindeer with him. And it was Mikkal's parent's hired man.

"*Buorre beaivi* – hello."

Sire Andaras was so surprised that he only barely mumbled his *Ipmel atti* – may God grant.

"Well, well, is it you," Gonge says.

"Yes," says Mikkal's parent's hired man to Sire Andaras, while he points at the earmarks on the four reindeer. "This is surely your mark and the animals came to us fourteen days ago."

"Yes, it's my mark," says Sire Andaras, and as the village man he was he added: "And that is the way it is registered in the records."

In a way, Sire Andaras could not be other than happy to have gotten these reindeer back again; but at the same time he thought that Mikkal and his parents wanted to pretend to be honorable people in this way, because Sire Andaras was a member of the town board and father of Elle.

The unfamiliar hand was entertained, and now it turned out in such a way that he and Elle came to talk together alone. He took a little paper slip up from the chest of his coat and handed it to Elle – and was supposed to say hello from Mikkal.

And Elle went into the woods and read: *Ráhkis Eližan* – my dear Elle – God's blessing and peace, and sincere greetings from me who is a bad person; but I am not so bad as people say. I have probably not had the fear of God; but when I think of you, then I have a need to be converted – to our benefit and to God's honor. And I hope to get to see your eyes this Easter. But then you will probably ride with Andi Piera's stallion, and you are too proud to look at me who is a bad person, and I don't know whether I will travel down to the village at Easter, because I am sorry at heart. But I, a poor human, send you my greeting in Jesus' name, amen. Mikkal. This pitiful piece of paper I found in the hymnal, and in the bag I found a pencil; I bought it at the Bosekop market last year. And my hand trembles when I am unworthy of you. And I want to become god-fearing – will see how it goes at Easter. Mikkal with a hearty greeting with the Holy Spirit. Mikkal. See psalm 51.

54

Mikkal and his parent's hired man stayed here until the next day; he spent the night in the servant's tent, with Gonga and *hoammá* Aslak.

Elle tore out the title page in the bible stories and went to the woods, made a pen from a juniper branch, warmed up a bit of frozen blood in her mouth and wrote:

Dear *Mikkalažan*. I thank you so sincerely for the letter and am so sorry that you say I am proud. No, I will never again ride with Andi Piera's stallion, even if the stallion carried his head twice as high. And you are not a bad person, and my heart is with you. And be god-fearing, dear *Mikkalažan*. And just come down to the village at Easter, and I will show everybody, both in this district and other districts, that I don't care what people say about you. And you are as good as anyone; my heart is with you. And I have cried because I rode with Andi Piera whom my heart loathes. But it was a sleigh ride, and I didn't know what I was doing. And when you wish God's blessing and peace for me, then I wish you the same with the Holy Spirit. See psalm 137. Your dear, dearest Elle. For I want to be your beloved if your heart is in the mood for me. And you can show everybody that you have become god-fearing and everyone will get to know that you have sent us all four reindeer. It isn't everyone who would have done that. And it did my heart good that you sent us the four reindeer, and one was a doe. Come to me at Easter, and we will go into the storehouse, you and I, and that everyone can gladly see. Greetings with the Holy Spirit – Elle, in love.

◆

Over there in the other valley Mikkal sat behind the tent and read Elle's letter. And he reached a decision: he would get religion – could see how it turned out at Easter. He could not hide from the others that, now and then, he had to smile from happiness; willy-nilly he could even break into a great laughter. And the happiness made him weak and loving in his knees and heart.

And it was just like that with Elle too. So strangely delightful to know that the body becomes loving and weak from thinking about Mikkal, and also when she doesn't think about him; indeed, when it is somehow just the body that thinks.

***

One day in March a man came driving up the wooded slope – the dogs ran down barking. Sire Andaras first thought it could be Andi Piera – and Elle thought that also for sure, for her face suddenly became so distended.

But it wasn't Andi Piera – it was just one of these poor, long legged Sámi farmers with the narrow faces – one of those who never bought reindeer, but nevertheless ate reindeer meat year round.

Now, he of course had to be entertained, whoever it was – his name was *Heaika Nillá* – Nils Henriksen – this man from the banks of the water.

They sat in the tent and ate and talked far and wide, and then *Heaika Nillá* says:

"And yesterday the sheriff came down to the village with Mikkal."

The others' faces rose in silent excitement. Elle's eyes stared – she stared straight ahead – without seeing anyone.

"Yesterday, you say?" says Sire Andaras, in order to just say something. "And who is it that has reported him?"

"Marit Ganda's son. He had gotten witnesses that Mikkal and his companion had taken that reindeer that had become lost to Marit Ganda last fall."

Elle barely managed to stagger out. As a sleepwalker she walked up over the wooded slope – it was easy to walk here – the snow had been tramped down everywhere and dug up by the herd; in their places one could walk as on rutted roads. Elle felt tender in her body, but it was another tenderness than the one she felt when she got a letter from Mikkal. This was so tender and painful; it was as if her head knotted up. From when she walked out of the tent her face had been stiff and hard until now. But now something burst in her chest, and she sobbed, aloud and helplessly. It didn't help much to try to believe that Mikkal was innocent; no, he probably wasn't innocent. But he had done it last fall, when it still hadn't dawned on him that he should get religion – for her sake. But how many reindeer Sámi were there actually who could say that they had not slaughtered an unfamiliar reindeer? Not to mention the long-legged ones from the banks of the water.

⋅

The others sat in the tent. *Heaika Nillá* says:

"And attorney Toddy-Jacobsen can be so big and legally trained and resourceful as a man can be; yet he will never be able to get Mikkal acquitted."

"He has gotten worse men acquitted than Mikkal," says Gonge. And Gonge is nearly bulging with arrogance on the part of attorney Toddy-Jakobsen.

"But it will depend on the chief magistrate himself too," says Sire Andaras. "He can question in such a way that a thief is suddenly sitting there as in a fox trap."

Heaika Nillá pulled a bottle up from the chest of his coat and handed it to Sire Andaras.

"Not on your life am I going to have some," said the citizen – it was obvious that *Heaika Nillá's* act was to waken liquor sweat with the host – and then include conditions as the spirits' demands increased.

"Well, when you don't want any yourself," said *Heaika Nillá* – "then I'll stick the bottle in the jacket again" – and did so. Gonge and *hoammá* Aslak looked as if they, in their greatest need, were being denied the sacrament.

But *Heaika Nillá* still tried to put on a good face opposite Sire Andaras and said that his errand naturally was to buy a reindeer for butchering.

"Yes, you can buy a reindeer for meat of course." And Sire Andaras winked at Gonge, slyly smiling.

"And what do you get for an ordinary reindeer bull?"

"Twenty-two kroner."

"Is that so – twenty-two. But I don't have that much money."

"No, no," said Sire Andaras, "it's expensive to buy a reindeer for slaughter. And frankly speaking, I don't know of more than six-seven families down in the village that buy reindeer meat. But the others are not lacking reindeer meat either." … "Yeah, there are even the others who wear the finest reindeer coats that are so shiny black that you could be mirrored in them. They no doubt had leg skin to choose between, those folks."

Heaika Nillá struck his large, long sheath knife into a wood block, straightened up where he sat, and said while staring fiercely at Sire Andaras:

"You can be certain that you'll get a beating when you come down to the village."

"I take you, Gonge, and you, *hoammá* Aslak, as witnesses to what *Heaika Nillá* says here. We have a sheriff and laws too in this district."

"I didn't say that I myself will beat you up. But the law doesn't prevent me from telling others how you discuss us down there in the village. And we don't usually let that sort of thing disgrace us without a reckoning."

It had already become evening, and *Heaika Nillá* made an expression that he wanted to travel down again; but he noticed very well that for Gonge it meant his soul's release from great privation to get to talk with *Heaika Nillá*. And he got it too. Then *Heaika Nillá* hitched up and drove down the wooded slope.

Gonge was supposed to have night watch of the herd, and he went up to the wooded slope. He captured one of his own reindeer bulls and went down from the slope. A couple miles later he met *Heaika Nillá* who was sitting there waiting for Gonge. *Heaika Nillá* overturned the sled, and they sat on it to drink from the bottle. Gonge agreed to sell the reindeer bull for five kroner; and *Heaika Nillá* corked the bottle again

"Another swallow – as cheap as I have sold – almost for nothing."

Heaika Nillá laughs full throated and shakes Gonge cheerfully:

"Well, Gonge, there's about half left in the bottle, you see. Walk up on the slope now, and then come back with a one-year-old reindeer." And *Heaika Nillá* laughs with open mouth. "It makes no difference if you go wrong and cannot distinguish your own mark from the others, now in this darkness – ha-ha-ha-ha! Take another gulp! – And, one more! … Yeah, what difference does it make if you should make a mistake!"

"Now, and if I actually did it, then …" and Gonge laughs a little shamefaced.

"Yeah," *Heaika Nillá* says, "you, who were such a cheerful rascal in the old days! Who cares, damn!"

Gonge took his skis and headed up the slope. But when he had come to the herd and had taken the lasso off it was as if he woke up … should he dare make a mistake? Now he remembered clearly his practical jokes in the old days, when he didn't have second thoughts, when this sort of thing was planned. But that was now so long ago … no, he didn't think he was able "to make a mistake" … On the other hand, it was too bad to take one of his own 2-3 reindeer. But *Heaika Nillá* was sitting down there, and Gonge hadn't tasted *jugástat* and straight alcohol since last year, lived practically speaking only on meat broth and meat. It burned so excruciatingly in his chest. The herd lay resting, spread out in the snow now at night time. By chance Gonge's own one-year-old reindeer lay there right in front of him; it wrung his heart, but it would have to go in God's name. He wound up some of the lasso and threw it.

◆

Heaika Nillá was downright shocked that Gonge had taken his own year-old reindeer. Maybe he was sorry for Gonge too; but mostly he was annoyed that there somehow was something wrong.

Gonge slept his drunkenness off in the snow this winter night.

The annoyance over Gonge's fickleness got *Heaika Nillá* excited. *Heaika Nillá* went up the slope and stole a one-year-old reindeer with Sire Andaras' mark – it was sort of his duty to do it now. And it was just cowardice that Gonge had taken his own. And Sire Andaras shouldn't have come out with his gloomy talk today for nothing, toss brazen accusations right at his face, *Heaika Nillá*.

***

Elle had sat up a long time on the slope. The painful message about Mikkal had distorted her otherwise so beautiful features; she felt it herself and was ashamed to go down to the tents again. But there she had to go. Sire Andaras knew well that she had been crying. Elle says:

"Now the bishop and the district governor will come. It would be fun to see the bishop's visitation in the church."

"But less fun for you to see Mikkal be sentenced," Sire Andaras was uncontrollably hard in his voice.

"Just as much; but I want to go down to the village now," and Elle too had gotten cold in her voice.

Konfirmánttat
Candidates For Confirmation

A couple days later they drove off. Actually, Gonge should have had his turn down to the village; but Sire Andaras was supposed to meet in the township board – so Gonge had to wait; but in return he was going to be able to celebrate Easter in the village. Sire Andaras would come to the reindeer camp before.

Sire Andaras had a small string behind him, a couple of reindeer each with a cargo sled with meat in it. And besides as usual an extra reindeer that was tied to the last sled. It was essential already now that they were driving north over the slope. It held back the last sled, probably not so that the sled would not run between the legs of the reindeer pulling the sled. But reindeer sometimes do that, and the string is tightened always when it is carrying a load down a slope. Elle too had to remember a laughable sight she had seen here before Christmas one time: Jouna Jouna and his little wife had come driving with a string, but had no extra reindeer behind. And now when they were going to go down a cleft in the road in the mountainside hill near the village headland the little wife had to act as the extra reindeer; she struggled and kicked against it all she could. But the sled jerked her over, pulled her along at full speed. Now she lay on her stomach, now on her back; in the next instant the whole string was bunched together, the reindeer and the sleds and Jouna Jouna and his wife on each other. And in the yard of the Sámi farmer Piera Hansa people stood laughing.

+

Sire Andaras and Elle drive down the ice onto the river; but where drifting snow has piled up tall, narrow mounds of snowdrifts, the sled road from before Christmas goes up into the scrub thicket – and down again – and then up again – now all the way up into the wooded slope. The valley up here is narrow, in places canyon-like; large ice blocks are overturned onto each other. Down in the steeper rapids in the river there are open channels and blue-green and yellow patches of ice. There is sunshine now in March, and up on the slopes the pine-

63

woods shine light green in the sun. But here at the bottom of the valley there is a little frosty fog. White ptarmigans glide scurrying and cackling through the willow bushes along the shore.

Then they come down to a group of cabins and a little below they turn into the only farm up here in this valley. Here the old hunter Beski lives, and Beski who is over 6 feet tall has a wife who in spite of her 70 years even today can keep up with the most active youth in a race. Their son Bojan is also an active fellow, but ungodly lazy; his mother usually intensifies her demands on him by challenging him to a race, and Bojan who is a little strange in manner can't stand that. Then afterwards she begins chopping wood so that the chips fly. Sire Andaras immediately set up a prize, an entire reindeer back. The old one ran and flapped with long trotter leaps and came to the finish line panting and wild-eyed. And it wasn't just as a bluff her son Bojan let her win; for Bojan had a little screw loose, and always lived in the belief that now the time had come when the old lady had to declare him the boss in the race. Afterwards they all sat in front of the fire and ate and laughed and drank many cups of wonderful coffee.

✦

They drive one and a half *beanatgullan* (distance at which a dog can be heard); three miles down, the two rivers bump together into large ice-covered rapids and form a stagnant, now ice-covered pool below.

They adjoin the sled road that comes from the western valley. Elle who is driving behind, stopped the reindeer; she has to sit and look at this sled road … here Mikkal had come driving a few days ago in the company of the sheriff. It twitched in the corners of her mouth, and Elle's eyes became large and stiff where she sat and looked at the furrowed, round grooves from Mikkal's sled.

✦

The valley became wider; a bit farther down were the main cabins. But the wooded hillsides and the river basin still had something of a mountain district about themselves. However, just below the main cabins the ice on the river began to go zigzag, between the flat and similarly formed river headlands with outlying meadows and birch woods and such. It continues the 12 miles to the village.

There was only a little twilight left when they drove up through the gap in the road in the innermost part of the village headland.

No, the world was no longer as it had been, Elle thought. Now that they drove through the upper part of the village. Then they stopped in the yard of Erki Lemik Issak where the many old storehouses stood.

"Do you have any *limpu* for me?" Sire Andaras asked Erki Lemik Issak who was standing there chopping wood.

"Yeah, for you I certainly have."

Limpu are solid clumps of reindeer moss with a birch twig stuck through.

***

Late the same evening when people had already begun to go to bed, Elle walked up and down past the courtroom's two detention rooms with the horizontal elongated small bars up high. It was dark, and no one passed this footpath in the snow at this time of the day. She stopped again and again: should she chance a shout to Mikkal? Just quite low. No, she didn't dare; but then she did it anyway, before she knew it herself.

"Mikkal! ... Mikkal!" ... Elle's heart beat so it was nearly breaking.

Then a face came into view in the one little barred window, a face from the doomed shadow world of the dead. Elle tried to smile, instilling confidence in him.

"I will wait until you are free," she says half whispering, "I want to be yours, if you want to have me, Mikkal!"

She saw that Mikkal stroked himself over his eyes. Then she heard steps, boot steps on the hard packed snow behind the courtroom corner. She fled her way like an arrow shot. Jørgensen the sheriff's deputy came ambling around the corner. Elle was way too far away for Jørgensen the sheriff's deputy to have a chance to be able to overtake her for a nocturnal meeting. That Jørgensen the sheriff's deputy always made a heavy effort with that sort; he would never succeed in getting a liberating success. He was immediately certain that Elle had had a conversation with Mikkal.

✦

Jørgensen the sheriff's deputy took his boots off and silently let himself into the courtroom, snuck up to the dark garret above the two detention rooms and lay down on the floor and listened. Then he lets out a little owl screech, is silent, then whistles a hymn melody, is silent again. He scratches the floor, lets it become quiet, gurgles a sound, quiet again. ... Then he hears a heavy groaning down in the detention room. He heard Mikkal say very clearly with a helpless voice: "Lord Jesus, save me from this evil!"

✦

The day after, Mikkal begged to be released from arrest. He wouldn't run away: he asked so pitiably for it and took God as witness that he would not run away.

And what good would it do to run away, run away where? Wasn't it enough that he had been served with a summons to appear in court? No, it was awful to sit in dark detention. It was dismally haunting in the empty courtroom during the night; he would go crazy, if he had to lie there one night alone. Finally, he asked in his desperation whether Jørgensen the sheriff's deputy didn't know anyone he could arrest as a comrade for Mikkal. Good God, there were so many who had stolen reindeer, so it shouldn't be difficult to find one who, with sufficient grounds, you could put under arrest. Jørgensen the sheriff's deputy didn't think there was anything in what Mikkal was speaking about, but he would see whether there wasn't one hole or another up in the dark garret, and that an eagle or some other animal could come through.

✦

Jørgensen the sheriff's deputy who didn't have much to do here in the village during spring and summer, usually went down to a fishing station by the coast at Easter where he ran a small business. But it was said that he never bought more than a couple hundred kilos of cod at a time – caution is a virtue – and then only when the cod didn't cost more than a few cents a kilo. He also ran a little shop trade there and sold water from his pump to the fishermen, ten cents a pail. And took ten cents so that one could be allowed to sharpen a knife on his whetstone. But last year there were a couple fishermen who not only refused to pay ten cents for a pail of water. No, they took Jørgensen the sheriff's deputyand tossed him into the sea. Jørgensen was able to crawl up again and ran home for his life when he saw that he was being followed. He jumped in through an open window when the door was too far away; but one of the fishermen got hold of his feet, and there the sheriff's deputy hung and screamed for help like a stuck pig.

Now before the court session he went around in the village, big and swinging his hips and black bearded. He also had one or another girl or woman in the farms in the area to sew Sámi shoes and such as goods for himself. Now he went around to see how the work was going, but actually to find fault with some of the work and material to be able to reduce the price, and at the same time to satisfy the women and girls and haggle and haggle.

***

The bishop, a large, stout and dignified gentleman, had of course gotten lodging at the parsonage, the district governor and chief magistrate with the sheriff. Attorney Toddy-Jakobsen who was just as good in the law as the district governor, and the other lawyer who was not Asper, Andijn's ill-fated fiancé, was staying at the businessman Hooch's. If one didn't know better, then one might be in doubt as to who was Hooch and who was bishop. The bishop also said to Hooch: am I Hooch, or is it you who are bishop? And Hooch said: it might in any case maybe have been most correct that I was bishop. Both had gray chin beards, eagle noses, large, distended eyebrows and thin white hair stroked up the same way.

So there was a vast crowd of big shots; never seen the likes! The village's male population seems to have put aside all work. They flocked together to the central courtyard and discussed who the various big shots were. And Juhas Juhasj said:

"And now, damned if the doctor isn't coming too. Yeah, may the Lord condemn Juhas Juhasj, the forest master is coming too!" The most congenial and popular of them all, a discreet father of one child or other near this long watercourse that stretches 150 miles down to the mouth in the northeast. The friend of the animals and the poor was the stout jovial forest master with the heavy moustache and in the green uniform, and no one actually seemed to resent that the forest master also was the friend of the girls. And in one case or the other he always did right and made a distinction even if there were no demands for it. "I shall say to you, my dear Per," he could say, "that Marit is the best girl you can marry … Yes, isn't that so? And here you have one hundred kroner to begin with, so you two can even get married tomorrow. Just as well to jump in as to crawl in, as the old ones' wise adage says. Yes, good luck to my dear young friend," and the kind hearted forest master managed to be able to wipe a tear from his cheek.

◆

"So he is always, the forest master," says Juhas Juhasj. "But Jørgensen the sheriff's deputy! What a scoundrel! He has no sense for gentlemanly behavior as Hooch and the others. But dicker for ten øre, that he can do! And he is supposed to be a Norwegian gentleman! Yes, see there he goes! Big and swinging his hips and black bearded, and with that loose, parrot-like nose tip always jerking in towards his jaw. He's always drifting around in the village and cheating the poor girls and women out of some coins. And he always wants to barter with them inside the small bedroom, in order to get a little lovemaking on the sly."

That's how Juhas Juhasj talked out there in the yard, along with a few others, a tall slim man with a long narrow face, fair skin, with long front teeth and high crooked nose. He was actually one of these insignificant people from the northeastern part of the village, but had parted with the reindeer thieves there, had married a girl from a better family and had worked his way up. "Yes, Juhas

Juhasj will probably end up as a well-off man," said people in the northeastern neighborhood; they were proud of him because he was counted among the respectable people in the village.

And the bigwigs were discussed inside out. That bishop they now had in the Troms diocese was supposed to be the second most important bishop in Norway, next to the Christiania bishop. And Erki Lemik Issak who also was standing here had heard that the Christiania bishop knew the entire book of Samuel in Hebrew by heart. And the district governor they now had was so rich that he could buy the largest wholesale business in *Opmerfeasta*; but he would rather be the district governor up here to be able to propose bills for the king and parliament, and that could be suitable for us up here. It was real gold he had on his district governor uniform.

***

Although it was a weekday, the bishop visitation had filled the church to the last seat. The bishop stood in the choir door in silk cassock and with a gold cross on his chest, handsome and tall and dignified. His deep sonorous voice could well have been a voice from the desert or a voice from heaven. Both the minister and the district governor who were also in the church felt impressed by this man, although they knew that the man was from a little mountain farm in Vestlandet somewhere and had originally been a student at a teacher's college. But they knew too that the bishop was a learned gentleman in the area of church music, was a good hymnist and had also written some hymns in Sámi.

Among the two rows that were going to be examined there was one person that towered an entire head above all the others, son of Benne, who recently had moved in from the Western Plateau district, the big taxpayer with over two thousand reindeer and money in the bank and gold and silver in the chest in the storehouse. Benne's son was eighteen, unconfirmed and still had trouble reading silently. But like the real *hoammá* he was he looked grand. His reindeer coat and the rest of his outfit really looked conspicuous in this gathering, as resplendent as primitive, bedecked with yellow, red, blue and green ribbons zigzagging around the enormously high upright collar and around the chest opening and the sleeve edges. And the wide leather belt was tightly covered with silver and brass buttons. And on it hung a large sheath that the knife shaft with a lead border stuck up from. He could not yet read right, as said; but now that he had come to this district he had become eager to get caught up on what had been neglected and was daily with little Olle, Ville Jongo's son, to get assistance. He was supposed to get married soon and had to be confirmed this spring, whatever it cost.

A little smile came over the bishop's face when he stopped in front of Benne's son.

"David who is mentioned in biblical history – who was he?" – The sexton repeated the question in Sámi.

"David? Yes, he was *gonagas*, king, and his son was Absalon."

Benne's son stood erect and spoke in his cheerful *hoammá* dialect.

"And Absalon rode on a horse through a forest and his hair got stuck in a *terebinth* – and the horse flew on, and Absalon hung between heaven and earth."

"*Terebinte*, you say?" says the bishop. "That word is not in biblical history."

"But it was *terebinte* I've heard."

The bishop's smile became somewhat jovial.

"Yes, that is quite right; *terebinte* was the name of the tree."

"Yes, *terebinte*, yes," says Benne's son. "*Terebinte*."

He had been suddenly concerned with what kind of tree it could have been, this *terebinte*; but perhaps it wasn't possible to ask the bishop. But fortunately Benne's son got hold of the thread again, and then his high *hoammá* voice thundered out again:

"And the king was saddened and said: Absalon, my son, my son!"

"Here it is said that David had in mind to build the Lord a house."

"Yes, and in that house Jesus was born, our savior who was crucified and arose on the third day from the dead and went to heaven and sits at God's right hand."

The bishop patted him on the shoulder and Benne's son felt gladly assured that the minister would confirm him, and then he could get married over Easter. It was urgent for Inga's sake.

Olle was, to begin with, proud on his behalf; but when he saw that the others were laughing he became a little embarrassed. He caught sight of Elle down there – so beautiful and grieved! No, never had Elle been so beautiful as now when she was grieved; and he got the idea that it was nice to be grieved, as Elle was now for the sake of love, and because Mikkal had acted badly and sat in detention and was going to be judged.

But at this moment something happens: Elle catches sight of Anga, the sorcerer's daughter. And Olle sees that Elle's face is transformed; she is no longer beautiful. It suddenly looks bewitched. No, Olle couldn't grasp it immediately; his young man's brain worked, and then he remembered that Mikkal was sitting together with Anga on the storehouse steps on the second day of Christmas, and that Elle had walked past and seen them. But Elle had also acted badly by driving with Andi Piera. And Jørgensen the sheriff's deputy who was sitting on the men's side down below, had also looked angry when he saw Anga and Mikkal sitting there on Christmas day. Olle couldn't take his eyes off Anga, Ågall's daughter, who had a gruff look and was so tall and slim. But he understood nothing from this face; it was as if closed. And on Elle's behalf Olle got such a dread for Anga's face; such a closed face is a dangerous face. And this sort of thing happens in the Lord's sanctuary during hymn singing and sermon from a great bishop in holy silk clothing that the two most beautiful girls suppress each other's soul and heart. Here in the church they fight in their thoughts over Mikkal who is now in detention. Only Anga's face still sort of wanted to say something! And if the bishop knew it, then with his deep, beautiful voice he would speak to Anga and Elle and ask them not to be evil toward each other. And Anga would say to Elle: Elle, you have the right to marry Mikkal. And Anga would cry because she has been good. But Anga's face went on being closed. The bishop's voice sounded like a voice from heaven or like a voice from the desert, and everyone sang so beautifully and loud today, because the bishop sang so beautifully and loud. He sang with a male angel's voice.

People streamed out of the church and stopped on the church hill. Elle didn't stop; she took the main road upwards, and the side road higher, up to Erki Lemik Issak's dállu, farm. Anga didn't stop either; she went down the hill to the sheriff's dállu, on the hill right on the south side of the church. She and her father were staying at the old sheriff's. Jørgensen the sheriff's deputyhad tried to catch Anga's glance and Elle's glance, but they had both held their glance away.

Now all the people both on the church hill and from the windows in the farms farther up see that the new chief magistrate is out walking with Andijn, Hooch's daughter. The chief magistrate is a bachelor, and people are attentive. But they don't think this magistrate amounts to much. A little low in stature he was and his feet pointed up when he walked. His eyes were long, but not good and his smile in the smoothly shaved face wasn't good either; it didn't help how extremely much he smiled. Via the coachman people had learned that he had not been friendly with some of the other gentlemen during the trip up. There had been a number of disagreements in the inns down in the valley.

* * *

In the afternoon the courtroom was full of people. In the morning there had been, as the village resident citizen Sire Andaras said, civil matters and now they were going to tackle criminal cases.

Jørgensen the sheriff's deputy stood there in polished, oil-tanned leather boots and frock coat, with a large starched shirtfront sticking up from the strongly low-cut vest; he was ordered to fetch Mikkal. He opened one of the detention doors that led right into the courtroom, and Mikkal walked up to the bar. The audience consisted mostly of the neighboring adults and fair-haired Sámi farmers from the northeastern part of the village.

"Your full name?" asks the magistrate.

"Mikkal Aslaksen Vuobme, born the seventh of March, 1860."

The audience smiled. People here as a rule usually don't know on which day they were born, barely in which year.

"Have you been sentenced?"

"Not quite; I was acquitted two years ago."

"Because of lack of evidence?"

"Yes, and I was innocent."

"You are accused of having stolen a reindeer around the middle of November last fall belonging to reindeer owner Lars Klemetsen Guttorm. Do you admit your guilt?"

"Guilt?"

"Yes. Do you admit that you stole the aforementioned reindeer?"

"But who can be witness to that?"

"Yes, you will get to hear that later. I am asking whether you admit that you stole the aforementioned reindeer?"

"That reindeer I slaughtered that time was my own."

"You plead not guilty then?"

"The law does not forbid one from slaughtering ones own reindeer?"

"And you therefore have not stolen the aforementioned reindeer?"

"One can surely not steal ones own reindeer?"

"How many reindeer do your parents own?"

"Well, about a couple thousand."

"You are therefore very rich people."

"Yes, according to the situation here we must be said to be that."

The magistrate dictates: the accused denies having stolen the aforementioned reindeer. The counsel for the prosecution acted as a sort of clerk of court.

The people in court could not refrain from looking at Mikkal. Mikkal was a little small of stature; but he had a surprisingly fine and dignified countenance and an elegant posture.

Utsahaš, who was the main witness against Mikkal, was very vacillating in his testimony. Yes, he had probably passed Mikkal's parents' *siida*, last fall up in the western valley and seen a couple of hides the ears had been cut off. And when he rode from this *siida*, he took a little round on skis a ways down, and completely by chance he noticed something in the snow. It was a couple of cut off ears.

"And that had Lars Klemetsen Guttorm's earmark?"

"Yes, that's what I thought at the time; but I can't be certain it was Guttorm's all the same."

"Do you know Guttorm's mark?"

"Yes, but there are so many marks; in this parish alone there are at least forty."

The counsel for the defense, stout Toddy-Jakobsen, was astonished how Jørgensen the sheriff's deputy had hit on holding Mikkal in detention. All that while where there was no reason whatsoever to think that Mikkal was going to flee or wanted to avoid showing up in court. By accident he had also heard something that was embarrassing to mention here; but as Mikkal's defender he felt obliged to do it. And in conferring with Mikkal and others who were aware of it this morning, he had become confirmed in his conviction that the rumor spoke the truth. Yes, it was this matter of the two girls. But – and Jakobsen's toddy-face blushed – he had heard something from Mikkal that overshadowed everything else: who has first, or more correctly said, who has had the opportunity to pretend to be a ghost in the dark garret above the detention room? It was nevertheless just one, Jørgensen the sheriff's deputy man, who had the keys to the courtroom and the detention rooms. Mikkal should be given the opportunity to describe the nature of the haunting to the court.

Jørgensen the sheriff's deputy shook and wanted to explain himself. But the magistrate who had become bewildered believed that this did not concern the case at hand.

The defense counsel believed that this was the pith of the case when all is said and done.

There was a great fuss. Toddy-Jakobsen had done something unheard of: turned against his own, against the authorities, even if in this case it just concerned Jørgensen the sheriff's deputy – had the attorney drunk too many toddies this morning? The audience gaped, the magistrate gaped, the counsel for the prosecution too – the old red-bearded sheriff who was Jørgensen's uncle didn't want to believe his own eyes and ears: what in the world was going on with Toddy-Jakobsen? Could it really be that he was right, but that sort of thing the authorities usually straightened up between themselves; you didn't settle things right before the public's eyes.

The handling of the case was put off until the following day. The public, the long legged ones from the northeastern part of the village, who to begin with had awaited with eagerness that it would turn out bad for Mikkal, the rich man's son: all of them became enthusiastic that now Jørgensen the sheriff's deputy would finally get his comeuppance!

And already the same evening the whole village had heard that there was haunting in the detention room and that Mikkal had been scared out of his wits. At the old sheriff's, where Ågall, Anga's father was living, there were plenty of people that evening. Ågall was not to be seen; no one knew where he was. People said many bad words about Jørgensen the sheriff's deputy; but soon everyone seemed to be in agreement that there had been evil spirits afoot. By no means to punish Mikkal; Mikkal was no worse than the others. But already for a long time it had smoldered here in the village. Andijn's fiancé who had already been underway to get married, had to turn around because of an evil will. First Christmas day Guta Lasse had been assaulted by evil spirits when he had come out into the entry of the church ... then Ågall had been there. But people had too great a respect for Ågall to want to think that he would let loose such evil.

+

This evening it was Hooch's turn to have a party for the authorities. And the gentlemen, including the bishop and the district governor, sat and talked about the haunting in the garret above the detention room. Toddy-Jakobsen received unanimous reproaches for having brought about this scandal and having attacked Jørgensen on such a loose foundation. But Toddy-Jakobsen said only that he liked to be a martyr and made himself a new Toddy. Jørgensen the sheriff's deputy, who had been frightened after the scene in court, had sent word he wasn't coming. But he had been fetched by the prosecuting attorney and the magistrate, and he who otherwise had never been used to being shown any special attention, now felt like a bashful candidate for confirmation. The magistrate especially was busy giving this official redress. And it was Toddy-Jakobsen the magistrate had been especially unfriendly with on the trip up. Besides he let it show through that he was somehow at home here with the Hoochs, and demonstrated intimacy with Andijn, the daughter of the house.

Ville Jongo and the old township treasurer were also here; Hooch and the minister and the sheriff had made it a practice of having these two along in company. And the old sheriff sat there in his fine, black homespun jacket with decorated, erect collar and a couple of yellow and red cloth stripes along the shoulders. And he had a black tie and white, starched shirtfront; on his legs he had Sámi shoes and leggings. He was in truth a handsome and stately man, blond, tall, had straight, powerful legs, a high, crooked nose and a full, nicely clipped beard and artistically woven belt around his waist, woven by one of his four beautiful daughters. The bishop also said to the district governor: the old sheriff is the most stately gentlemen of us all and always tactful and amiable. He was a big shot in the village, had cows and horses and a lot of money in the bank – and 39 grandchildren who threatened to become a deluge for the old sheriff. But he took comfort that there could always come something good from a deluge of 39 grandchildren – and God's earth has use for many zeroes. Jongo on the contrary, though a good imposing man was a typical Sámi in shape; but it was he who had it in his head and fingers. He held a worthy speech and thanked the bishop and district governor and the other authorities together with the shadow of sickness, the doctor, on behalf of the village: "What you, my distinguished gentlemen, have achieved here ought not to be measured with a yardstick; for that matter, it could even be measured with the width of a finger. But we have seen you, seen the high spiritual and worldly authority in the unfolding of office, and that is wherein it lies. We want to see those who stand over us; and we find comfort that the high authority with its visit makes it clear to us that we too belong to society."

***

Late the same evening Elle stands behind the corner of the old sheriff's barn, and stares in the darkness to see whether anyone would come and stop on the foot path lying to the side that went past the detention wall. She had seen Anga, Ågall's daughter today. Elle was unable to read anything in her face; well yes, one thing: Anga didn't want to betray anything. And the other thing: Anga seemed to know that someone wanted – was dying to know – whether her face would betray something, and from that she had her joy to be sure, from the little smile at the bottom of the silent face. And what did Ågall want to do? He had much in his power, the man, could perhaps even save Mikkal from being found guilty. And it is this thought that makes Elle confused. She who would have been ready to sacrifice her life for Mikkal, now suddenly is addicted to a crazy idea: Mikkal perhaps has, when all is said and done, sincerely deserved to be found guilty and get his punishment … oh no, the authorities will not let themselves be duped by Ågall. Justice will run its course. And Elle feels a breeze in her chest, and when she again is clear over what she has thought – and seen the hopelessness in it, and that it anyways wouldn't help her, not release her from her love anguish – then her heart wrenches again. And before she realized it she hurries in her helplessness across the path, stops at the detention wall, and with her breath in her throat she shouts quite loud:

"Mikkal! … Mikkal! …"

And Mikkal's face comes into view in the narrow, barred window.

"If you are afraid that there will be ghosts, Mikkal, I will stand here."

Mikkal says something; she doesn't quite hear it.

Elle stood there until it began to get light in the morning.

***

The next day morning the court came into session again. Mikkal confessed and got a few months in prison in *Troandin*, Trondheim.

The audience, the long legged ones from the northeastern part of the village, were on the verge of jumping out of their skin, although to begin with yesterday they had wanted it badly that Mikkal be found guilty. But this business with Jørgensen the sheriff's deputy and the haunting … yes, also it was shocking that when Mikkal had had a chance of being acquitted, he goes and admits his guilt, out of dumb confusion! Mikkal, though, had not been very clever yesterday. But everyone was arrogantly in agreement that if *Heaika Nillá* had been in Mikkal's place then he would have wriggled away from it like nothing. But others thought that Mikkal had gotten religion in the detention room and had become a believer.

***

The next day the authorities departed. The magistrate and the two attorneys via horse down the valley, only to separate 20 miles above the river estuary; the attorneys were going to cross the isthmus on the east side and then continue along the north side of the long fjord to the east, each to his own town there. The closest of these towns lay 175 miles from the inland village here.

The bishop was going to the West Plateau district, in a southwesterly direction, and to there the hefty man had to ride in a reindeer sled – 110 miles to sit in a sled, first 55 miles up the valley here, spend the night in a mountain hostel by a large lake, then the next day over a massive plateau and finally the third day a ways up a mountain valley to the village there.

The magistrate was going with reindeer conveyance over the plateau to a larger market district at a fjord bottom in a west-northwesterly direction, and there it was 110 miles, to be sure, sheriff's miles. There were three mountain hostels on this stretch. All letter and package mail going to the towns and villages to the east was still driven during the winter on this road around the inland villages here and further down the valley; for during mid-winter there were no steamships going east more than once a month.

No, for this spry magistrate it was nothing to sit and ride in a sled, and he had the company of Mikkal who was going to Trondheim to serve his sentence; and the two of them had it quite nice during the trip over the plateau.

Finally, the shadow of sickness was going via horse over the low plateau on the north side of the valley – to his main district by the nearest fjord bottom. It was this road people here in the village drove up with their flour products – Russian flour in large eighteen stone Russian sacks, bought by the merchants on the coast from Russian cargo boats from Archangel, and that during the summer ran a tusk trade with the Norwegian fishermen – so many stones of pollack, so many stones of flour. And in the course of time a strange language arose, Russian Norwegian and that Norwegians and Sámi thought was Russian, while the Russians on their part really understood it as Norwegian. But it was a good, cash language. And as a rule they didn't write contracts – a word was a word – it lived as letters of fire until the following year; and if the skipper died in Archangel in the meantime, the word was just as hallowed for his descendants on the cargo boat.

But the people here in the rural area also used to drive in large reindeer caravans to the spring and fall markets at the fjord bottom to the west – and a few too, but just horse people, to a market held at the fjord bottom to the east.

***

The day after the authorities had traveled, Jørgensen the sheriff's deputy held an auction of a reindeer and a nearly new sled for tax arrears of Andi Lasse's widow – and it was outside a storehouse that she had had together with another mountain Sámi family at Piera Hansa's farmyard. There were many people present, and Andi Lasse's widow wept and complained, and when she was constantly in the way of Jørgensen the sheriff's deputy, he came to poke her and she fell down – and then it was Ågall, whom the sheriff's deputy hadn't noticed before, stepped forward and said:

"Pick her up, you, Jørgensen the sheriff's deputy."

Jørgensen flared up and said:

"You go to hell, Ågall."

It became deathly still. Everyone saw that Jørgensen had become white as a corpse and shook. But he tried to control himself and waved the hammer:

"Ten kroner is the offer for the reindeer – ten kroner – ten kroner …"

The hammer fell from his hand – he picked it up – ten kroner – the hammer fell from his hand again – Ågall's glance rested on him – ten kroner – again the cursed hammer falls from his hand, and now Jørgensen the sheriff's deputy is trembling like an aspen leaf.

"It is surely best you leave the hammer lying there. You can't hold it in your hand anyway," Ågall said in Norwegian.

"Ten kroner – ten kroner," and Jørgensen hit the storehouse steps with his fist.

The sheriff's deputy goes homeward, and suddenly there was someone who jerked him by the sleeve; and Ågall's owl face looks at him. Jørgensen had probably been walking in a reverie, since he hadn't heard anyone coming after him.

"Stand here a little," says Ågall – and Jørgensen stops.

"You were clever at scaring the daylights out of Mikkal."

"I?"

"Yes, just you, yes! And don't try to deny it, not face to face with me. But now I want to give you some good advice – and I will also advise you to follow it – just between you and me: you have nothing other to do than … well, anyway do as you want – for that matter take your pick."

The sheriff's deputy stands quivering and wants to walk on. Then Ågall whispered something to him in the ear and said that this would besides be between them.

◆

And the rumor started that Jørgensen the sheriff's deputy had locked himself into the detention room several nights in a row and moaned out loud when it began to get haunted up in the dark garret above the detention room. And this time it hadn't been an ordinary person who had knocked about up there. Yes, someone even said, true enough long afterwards, that a woman, Lemma Marit, had seen shadows of white grave clothes come from the cemetery that wasn't at the church but on a hill southeast of the village headland.

◆

However that may have been: Jørgensen the sheriff's deputy had in these days gotten a somber, pallid look, and there were those who felt sorry for him. And it was so that he had a good excuse to travel down the valley and to the fishing station out by the coast, where he had begun a little business. It was rumored that the capelin had been noticed in large quantities off the coast, and the cod wasn't far away either. Some of the young people also began to get ready to go out to the fishing grounds, but not to just any old station; it had to be a station where the sea Sámi usually fished, and with these they usually took spots as workers who shared the catch. Also from North Finland some Kvens came on foot with birch bark baskets on their backs when cod fishing grew near, and some of them settled down here in the country for good – half the population in the towns consisted of Kvens.

***

Easter was getting close. Elle was still here, and now that Mikkal had been sent to Trondheim, Andi Piera had gotten excited about his big, black stallion. An equal as a persevering suitor you would have to look for a long time. But Elle was now less than ever inclined to tolerate him. Well, Andi Piera would have to see how it would turn out this fall.

Ågall and his daughter were also still here; they wanted to celebrate Easter here. No, Elle couldn't help it; again and again she had to look at Anga, and never, never would she succeed in seeing what dwelt behind Anga's closed face. Just the one thing: Anga knew that someone really wanted to know that, but it was certainly not going to happen. Rumor had it that illnesses' shadow, the doctor, had begun to have her as an assistant down in the fjord district. He never thought he was able to do anything without having her help, and it was the first time people heard a doctor say that Ågall could cure certain illnesses. He felt reassured when he had her close by; but as soon as she was away the uneasy insecurity was again there. The doctor was a blue-eyed man with large, dark beard and glasses.

***

For businessman Hooch and his wife the assembly days had had an exhilarating effect. The new magistrate had been very strongly absorbed by Andijn, and it appeared that it had made an amusing impression on Andijn herself. But it was understandable enough that she wasn't immediately charmed by him; he wasn't really of that type, seemed perhaps also somewhat unpleasant. But there was no doubt that he had become strongly enamored of Andijn, and a magistrate was after all a magistrate.

78

Einar Asper had written a single letter to Andijn from Christiania this winter. In itself a moving, beautiful letter; he wrote that death would be preferable to walking in fear that this malignant tumor on the brain would make him a helpless living human being. And then he said in the letter, convincingly sincere: forget me, Andijn – you have life in front of yourself, and with me there is not life.

He had at the same time also written a letter to Hooch himself; in it he said that he was undergoing an examination by a specialist.

Hooch no longer thought he understood Asper. In the letter he wrote before Christmas – when he was on his way up here – it seemed quite simply to be evident that all this almost unbelievable sacrificing Asper had done exclusively to spare Andijn a breakdown – in and of itself, a rarely beautiful outcome from a fine person's way of taking on an affair of heart – he had clearly a living idea of what a terrible blow the glaring truth that time would have been for Andijn; it would have given her a blow for life.

But now, now a report comes – it came in the mail today – Einar Asper had had to undergo an operation for a tumor on the brain. The report comes from the town to the east; the brief, sober truth was that Einar Asper had had to undergo an operation for a tumor on the brain.

Hooch stands with the letter in his hand, and the first and only thing he says here where he stands is: oh, how life is still kind!

He tells it to his wife, and her face becomes lighter; she can hardly keep from smiling.

Carefully and alone with her, Hooch tells it to Andijn and shows her the letter from the town. And slowly and with difficulty it lights up in her countenance; she just doesn't know what she is thinking about. The whole livelong day she walks through the rooms of the house, takes a tour on the roads, bewildered and happy and perplexed … She awakens during the night, and then it dawns on her: she hadn't believed it was true what Einar wrote last fall when he was underway, when he turned back. And she thanks God that she didn't know, that she didn't believe – God had done it – that she, face to face with herself, could pretend she believed what Einar wrote.

And so Einar had told the truth anyway! My poor, poor boy! … Andijn was on the verge of saying: I will be faithful to you; I shall care for you; I shall be good to you, the same words she had said immediately before Christmas … Now she couldn't say it; she felt that it would sound false … so much had sunk to the bottom in the meanwhile, so much had been pulled up by the roots, and much had withered of that which could have bloomed.

***

Easter came with mild weather and radiant sunshine; the eaves were dripping.

Andijn went to see Halle Johanas, the fair, young Sámi with the cheerful, Norwegian face and who at Christmas had run his horse to death, because Andijn incessantly wanted to have the wild speed and because he couldn't refuse.

And Halle Johanas who now didn't have a horse himself borrowed a horse from a cousin, and Andijn and he had driven up the ice on the river on gliding conditions in the sunshine, with sleigh bells singing. Andijn's mood was like the Easter sunshine itself; she yoiked wildly, hummed and sang the small Sámi texts that hadn't been able to be shaped rhythmically, but nevertheless had a little of the verses' charm and elusive shyness about themselves.

♦

No, Hooch hadn't wanted to go along with giving Halle Johanas compensation for the horse that had been run to death at Christmas, not even partial compensation. Johanas had been responsible himself. Hooch was rather difficult in that way. And it had caused much indignation in the village, and Halle Johanas himself had swallowed many a bitter pill at the thought of it. But Andijn couldn't help it, and when Andijn was near him and he smelled the fragrance of her, it was as if a dewy whiff glided through his mind. To be sure it was so that as a man and owner of the horse he had had the responsibility himself.

Hooch was at this time irritable in a monetary way too because his son Fridtjof who was still in Archangel to learn the language had become more and more aggressive in asking for money. And in the letters Hooch could read between the lines that Fridtjof found himself in difficulties, steadily in greater difficulties, although he should almost have been able to manage with the wages he had. Hooch didn't want to show it to his wife; but he himself was certain that Fridtjof had wandered from the straight and narrow and that in earnest. This winter Hooch had said to himself that it would be good for God's bright angel to do some uninhibited messing around; but now Hooch had become worried. Fridtjof wasn't prepared to tolerate that sort of thing … Fridtjof was going to come home, that is, to the town to the east, as soon as the ice in the White Sea had broken up, sometime in May; he was going to come with a Russian flour cargo boat and begin at his grandfather's store in the town.

Dálvi II
Winter

It was past Easter now. Citizen Sire Andaras had paid taxes; the last township board meeting had been held; and everything that didn't have to go on the trip up to the *Gáisá* glaciers would be left in his storehouse that stood among the many old storehouses in Erki Lemik Issak's farmyard; and there were a couple of fine driving sleds, harnesses, a chest with silk shawls and gold and silver things in it, finest reindeer coats, finest homespun jackets and much more.

Elle had traveled up to the *siida* before Easter – a couple days after Mikkal had been sent away – so that Gonge could get relief and travel down to the village. And Gonge along with a few comrades from the West Plateau district had stood diligently at the counter in Hooch's country store and drank half-pint shots; yeah, how they had all been grand and rich. Gonge himself had once been a *hoammá*, and it was magnificent again to be able to be grandiose and boisterous.

But Gonge was more dead than alive, when one day after Easter he had to go with Sire Andaras and Zare to the *siida* up there in the valley.

***

And now they are again at their *siida*. It is already about the middle of April and time to depart.

There has been mild weather these days and a heaven's abundance of sun; the nights have already become bluish light. The snow on the pine branches has plopped down, and the snow piles around the pine trunks are new to look at; as opposed to the snow that the reindeer herd had tramped down in the course of the winter. Yes, it looks as if a market has been held here. And shed reindeer antlers lie everywhere on the wooded slope; some reindeer had already begun to shed antlers in the middle of March.

No sooner has Sire Andaras begun to untie the knots on the tent and pulled the first flap aside, than the dogs are certain as to what is at hand. And they immediately take the lead, bark and yelp and are in the way everywhere.

Zare, his wife, packs the homespun tent blankets down into a couple of the wide cargo sleds and Elle packs in all kitchen utensils and clothes and foodstuffs. Sire Andaras places the tent poles above the blankets, but the tent ears, the four curved and thicker main poles that are together in pairs and bear the cross poles around the smoke vent, he ties loosely on the side of the cargo sleds since it is awkward to have them on the load.

Their summer tents of barked canvas they have in a mountain cabin ca. 15 miles northwest of the Sámi farmer's summer pastures. They were left there last fall when they were on the move from the *Gáisá* glaciers to the north.

Gonge and *hoammá* Aslak have gone up onto the mountainside. They make a mile-wide round to get all the reindeer along, and the whole mountainside resounds of baying dogs.

Sire Andaras himself has fetched the draft reindeer; now there are just the hearth with a few stones and the bed of twigs left there.

The herd of a thousand odd reindeer comes whistling down from the mountainside; dog baying resounds; it crackles like small lightning pops in the toe joints of the animals. And the herd is nudged down onto the ice on the river.

Sire Andaras himself drives the string down from the mountainside. Down on the ice Elle has the string after her. Sire Andaras takes out his skis and follows the herd that moves in a long, narrow, wavy strip – just three to four wide. They keep the order in the ranks to avoid having to break a path as much as possible; those in the front can do that. Farthest forward is Gonge on skis with a bell reindeer on a lead, and now when everything is going like a streak, *hoammá* Aslak is at the rear in his sled. He is beginning to get old now, Aslak.

They have come out of this valley, and Elle takes a look up the valley in a southwesterly direction … and wonders whether Mikkal's parents have departed now, the rich ones …

They continue once more down the valley. A bit above the Sámi farmers' summer pastures by the same river, they head up the steep slopes on the north side. No, they don't stop before they are up on the high, flat mountain plateau. But here the herd, smelling reindeer moss beneath the snow, already stops on its own; the reindeer dig down to the moss in the heather, actually dive down and stretch out so that the hard snow crust flies around them. It is night, a light blue night of dusk. The people kindle a fire; they have pinewood with them from the mountainside. The herd will get to graze here for a good while. The reindeer are not very strong now in the spring; the spring change is in their bodies. Their antlers have been shed. Their hair layers are pitiful, and the bot fly larva between the hide and membrane have gotten quite annoying for a few reindeer; it burns large holes in the hide.

And here there are no fewer than two to three hundred pregnant cows, and they are all going to calve at the beginning of May. While most other of God's creatures mate in the spring, the reindeer's mating time is in November and this month is also called *ragatáigi*, mating season. As Sire Andaras once explained to the bishop:

"It is a result of He who keeps an eye on everyone's welfare will not allow the reindeer calves to come into the world at such a difficult time for them as for example in the fall or earlier in the spring. No, we decide on November as *ragatáigi* for the reindeer. But creatures that have acquired reason for their own use, they most often are allowed to do as they will, and since they often make mistakes, they learn to distinguish between good and evil, but that too is very good."

◆

Later in the morning it began to snow; but they departed and headed north. Elle took the road in a northwesterly direction with a couple of reindeer and a driving sled to pick up the summer tent that had been put in the storehouse last autumn at the first mountain hostel. Here a family lived; but this inn was not for winter travelers between the inland valley and the fjord bottom to the west – the winter road went farther north; no, it was just summer mail carriers and other travelers that this inn was intended for. Elle stopped here until later in the night when it had begun to clear up again and there was a chance of getting good, hard snow that she could drive across the plateau in the light blue night as on a rough ice surface. And later towards morning she caught up with the herd, some 12 miles north of *Geaidnojávri*.

They now took only a couple of short rests and continued on with the migration, in the hope of being able to reach a sheltered hollow with birch underbrush on the plateau to the north within a couple of days, not far from the *Gáisá* glaciers, before the cows began to drop calves.

But one evening the northeast storms took hold, and the sky and earth disappeared to the people's eyes; there was nothing else to see than snow-filled air that cascaded around them, blinded them, forced them to claw their way in where they were. The dogs had suddenly become wretched animals that just tried to save themselves and find the best places in the lee of the sleds. They didn't need to fear for the herd; there was no valley nearby that would tempt them; and when bad weather like this was beginning the reindeer knew that it was best to stay on the heights where the snow was steadily swept away, while the depressions were veritably buried.

The string and the people found themselves in a creek bed with a little birch underbrush; it was out of the question to set up the tent. They propped it up with a few poles just enough so that there could be room for five people. In there they lay and sat, and the dogs were left to find the best spots for themselves.

"Sulphur sticks are the only sticks that work," Gonge says, while he strives to get a fire started. "The new matches light up and go out as if you had spit on them … what next, this is like hell too!"

Here they sleep, here they eat. And when Sire Andaras wants to go out toward morning there is just a small hole in the snow on the lee side. He has to take veritable swimming strokes to come out and up. The storm has let up a little, and it is snowing less. He doesn't see a hint of the sleds, and although he thinks he should know where they lie he must nevertheless struggle for a long time back and forth before he finally feels a sled under his feet.

No, beginning to move again was out of the question, and one does as one does: you resign yourself to it. And they lie and sleep and eat and smoke.

"Many of those who usually migrate up to *Spierttanjárga*, a peninsula to the east," says Sire Andaras, "have now become parishioners in *Buolbmat* and no longer come to our district in the winter."

Sire Andaras tells everything to Gonge and *hoammá* Aslak both of whom are originally from the West Plateau district and have never been to the east.

"But have you ever," asks Gonge, "seen the Russian Sámi, the Skolt Sámi?"

No, Sire Andaras had not. But he could tell about other mountain Sámi to the east who were very rich; but their reindeer were small, much smaller than the reindeer here.

"But have you been to Enare in Finland?"

No, Sire Andaras hadn't; but he could tell that they were people from high places, even richer than the Sámi to the east; yeah, there was one by the name of Radele who had five thousand reindeer.

"My goodness!" exclaimed Gonge. "And there is inexhaustible grazing land there."

In the old days it was like that, Sire Andaras tells, that the Finnish Sámi could move to the Norwegian Sámi farmers in the spring, and the Norwegian

Sámi could let their herds graze in Finland during the winter. But the Russian government and the Norwegian government wrote common laws that this would not be allowed any longer. Which is good for us in the summer, but not in the winter. And for the Finns it is good during the winter, but not during the summer.

"Is it far to Enare?" asks Gonge.

"Yeah, it is quite far. We don't understand the Enare language; but it is nevertheless Sámi, it too. And we don't understand Skolt Sámi either. And further south in Norway and Sweden there are also Sámi that we don't understand. And they are very small and thin, have flat faces and small, black eyes, most of them – yes, as do many with us too – and they go in top hats. It is these people who have printed pictures in the books. But they cannot be Sámi as we are."

"Yeah, it's just they who are Sámi, probably," says *hoammá* Aslak who himself looks like a printed picture, lacks only a top hat.

Zare, Sire Andaras' wife, says to Gonge and *hoammá* Aslak:

"But you in the West Plateau district cannot sew clothing, you either. And their tents can simply be called fragile nests – from what I have seen."

"But we are big and fat," Gonge says and laughs, "and we are the ones who can yoik. And we are rich, and we are elegant, and we are handsome – and can do whatever in hell we want!" – And Gonge laughed like a big, tame troll here among Christian folks.

"I'm going to tell you," says Sire Andaras, "what the merchant bishop *Hooká* thinks about that thing. And the merchant bishop himself once was going to become an all-knowing doctor, so he should have some sense about it. The merchant bishop thinks that the Sámi in the West Plateau district are descended from Norwegian people and Swedish people – yeah, and from Finns. And the merchant bishop thinks that is why you in the West Plateau district go around in rotten reindeer coats and rotten footwear and have fragile nests for tents, because unlike the rest of us you have not inherited a sense for proper life on the mountain."

"But I've heard," says Gonge, "yeah, it is a Norwegian midwife who said it – that it is owing to life in the old days that there were so many big and fair people among the Sámi here in our parts."

"Yes," says Sire Andaras, "Norwegian men and Swedes, they have always been big adulterers."

"But heathens, they're adulterers, I've heard," says Gonge as if in a sort of deferential admiration and as if to trump the others, "it's big to be big – in whatever it is."

"Shut up!" says Zare.

◆

The next morning a south wind came with sunshine and threatened to destroy the conditions even up here on the plateau. But since this *siida* was out relatively early, they succeeded after a couple of days' energetic migration in reaching the cozy hollow southeast of the closest *Gáisá* glacier before the cows began to drop calves.

But those who were out late – on either side of these large and desolate plateaus – they had something else to contend with: slush up to their arms, ice on the lakes inundated with water, drifting ice and flooding in the rivers – children and pregnant women have to be saved – and in the middle of all this the calving begins.

... Sire Andaras' people had already gotten the camp ready when this occurred. The reindeer bulls had been separated from the herd of cows, so that they wouldn't trample the calves to death and be in the way, and *hoammá* Aslak was supposed to herd them in the meanwhile.

There were still only bare spots on the range of hills, the hollow that sloped toward the fjord bottom to the east. Along the creek bed it was rather dense with small birch and willow copse; but the creeping and sort of grown together dwarf birch was still completely covered by snowdrifts.

It began to swarm with small calves in the herd of cows. The people ran around continuously, day after day, since it was literally a matter of life for many of the calves. For the cow often has the tragic bad habit that it simply tramples its own young to death if it doesn't smell it in time. Then it dawns on her that it is her duty to take care of this creature. And it can also simply run off.

"Oh, damn it all! Look now!" Sire Andaras shouts, as pious a soul as he otherwise is. He runs with a fresh gaff hook in hand to a cow that just threatened to become murderous; he throws the lasso on the cow, hauls her to the calf, moves the calf in to the mother with the fresh stick – yes, for if the calf is touched by human hands before the mother has smelled it then she will one way or another not recognize it any longer. But now she gets to smell the calf without guilty decorum, and Sire Andaras can safely run on to save other calves from being killed under their mothers' hooves.

But here were also many cows that had not gotten pregnant.

Day after day the people move around, often eat standing or walking from the food they have in reindeer coats or homespun jacket pockets.

Then most of it had been gotten through, and there had come a new group of young into the herd. And only a quarter of a day old a reindeer calf can run so fast that a grown human cannot catch up to it. God, who considers everything, and he has a lot to consider, has also noticed that it is necessary for a reindeer calf to be able to flee from its pursuers as soon as it has come into the world.

But there were many calves that had succumbed in this hard world. They were flayed for the hide's sake – the hide of a newborn calf has such a fine hair layer. The color changes into lovely golden and brown; they become extremely lovely children's coats.

Zare says to her husband:

"Someone who had a little child … wouldn't you like that too. Andaras?"

"That will have to be God's matter," says Sire Andaras.

Those cows whose calves were dead were milked. But Elle and Zare could only milk ten to fifteen cows before the little wooden bowl, cut out of a burl on a birch trunk, could be filled. But that milk is also fatter than even goat's milk.

***

The nights now at the beginning of May had become quite light; and it wouldn't be long before the midnight sun could cross the earth's rim without touching it.

Now good days had come; Elle went one evening on skis up the heights to the west, up toward the closest *Gáisá* glacier. From a ridge below the glacier she had a great view to the east and west. She stood and listened as to whether barking dogs or migrating shouts could be heard. Mikkal's parents would now be underway here, if they hadn't already gone past. They had close to 60 miles still to walk – north over the long, large peninsula. They were going with the herd over the Magerøy sound; on Magerøy up to North Cape the herd could move around freely the entire summer. A long way to migrate now when the ice on the lakes was unsafe and the rivers difficult to cross. But then they would be able to sleep the entire summer too, when they had set up camp well on the shore by the sound.

Then Elle caught sight of a rough stripe far to the west, and it was moving northward, and she heard a distant sound of barking dogs. The stripe was long and large. Yes, that was probably Mikkal's parents migrating together with his father's stepson's family that wasn't rich, but the stepson was an honorable man. One can well be poor and an honorable man at the same time, for if one is born and grows up in the West Plateau district there are many honorable men there. But now Mikkal was sitting in jail in *Troandin*. He would get out at the end of August, come by steamship (*dámpa*), get off at the fishing station on Magerøy sound and find his parent's tent there. Now, old Vuabme, Mikkal's father, had surely been a rogue in the old days, according to what Elle had heard. And indeed it was: neither he nor his wife had become more bowed down when Mikkal was found guilty; annoyed they were to be sure, but startled and stunned, no way, although they were wealthy people and wanted to put on airs. Yes, perhaps they themselves hadn't eaten the meat of the reindeer that they knew full well Mikkal had stolen. It hadn't occurred to them to reproach him for having made himself guilty in a misdeed.

Elle had at this time begun to rebel both against herself and against Mikkal. He was handsome, had a warm attitude; and all Norwegians, both men and women, said that he resembled a prince. A bit small in stature, but his face was fine as if he should have been son of a government official.

The feeling of rebellion grew in Elle. True enough, Mikkal had been adored in his way: young people wanted to crowd around him. But Mikkal didn't seem to feel at home among decent people; and respected people didn't seem to value his company either.

… Elle continued up the rise to the closest *Gáisá* glacier. Here were many large *Gáisá* glaciers that could be seen all the way from certain level plateaus – 60 miles away – and there, from a distance, the glaciers looked like white swans with beaks under their wings.

Elle felt it as a remedy to be able to admit that she had had a rebellion, that she henceforth despised Mikkal: he can just as well go to hell, she said aloud.

And these violent and rebellious thoughts drove her involuntarily all the way up to the top of the glacier. Up here the sun and the red light of dawn flamed over the world that is desolate and high up. To the east and far below she saw their own two tents. A little blue smoke column rose from one of them. She saw the sea far to the north, and a little of the fjord to the east, and the steep, ragged mountain walls that climbed up from the sea farthest out on the east side of the mouth of the fjord. And down there lay the village at the fjord bottom from which the village people in the inland valley usually fetched their flour in Russian sacks on the winter roads.

Oh, now she saw quite clearly the stripe with Mikkal's parents' large herd, which was moving northward to the west. Oh, if Mikkal nevertheless hadn't done what he did … Then she wouldn't have been able to refrain from moving on … or Mikkal would have caught sight of her, or he would have come into their *siida* … here someplace they would have met … Elle felt a couple small nervous twinges in the corners of her mouth; she cried a little, couldn't help it.

There were also a couple other reindeer camps here in the *Gáisá* region, Jouna Jounas and Johanas Lasses: but they usually stayed far to the west.

But most Sámi were on the peninsula far to the east, and they usually didn't herd their reindeer during the summer.

When Elle came home, her mother was already boiling morning coffee. Elle told where she had been, and that she had seen a moving *siida*.

"That was probably Vuabme's people, probably," says her mother.

Sire Andaras lay snoring.

"Go and wake up Gonge, so we can get the cows milked before they begin to graze," says her mother.

Elle was so wonderfully in a good mood now; she slipped into the servants' tent without a sound. She took a wisp of hair and stroked it carefully and lightly over on the back of the hand of the sleeping Gonge. There were a couple of twitches in the big troll. She remained standing there bent over and observed him … he was a huge human – he was very imposing where he lay and slept. He had some powerful legs and arms, a large mouth; and Elle was convinced that this was the first time she looked at Gonge as a man. She wiped his mouth with the wisp of hair … Gonge turned his head and gesticulated with his hand. Then he awoke, and his sleep-drunk eyes suddenly were wide-awake, when he discovered that it was Elle who stood bent over him. She smiled, she laughed:

"Come and drink some coffee now, then we can go out and milk."

"You who are so clever at using the lasso, you must be able to take the cows yourself."

But Elle laughed and pulled him up. Gonge smiled; it was something undreamed of and new for him, this … He felt precisely that something new awoke in him, but still just in his head and heart.

And this was infinitely much more arousing than the morning coffee itself.

Hoammá Aslak who had been afraid of being dragged up from his blissful repose, he too, forced out the vital spirits: now, thank God, you got off easy from that!

And Elle had cheese in Gonge's coffee cup, the first cheese this year.

They went out to the cow camp, Gonge with lasso over his shoulder, Zare and Elle each with their round wooden bowl, widest in the middle, so the milk wouldn't splash out if the cow kicked.

Gonge coaxed: *gužža, gužža!* The reindeer like salt. He wound up the tarred, stiff lasso into small rings through a smooth hole in the antler loop on the one end and threw, and the cow dangled there. A couple of cows were besides so tame and happy to be milked that they came themselves and lined up.

Elle slept the entire morning – and yet didn't sleep. And when she got up, she asked Gonge whether he wanted to go along to the tarn below: there had already been, she said, a large open channel in the ice farthest down, where the brook empties, and it was just there that the trout and char hung out this time of year.

They found a few hooks, and Elle tied a piece of red yarn as bait on them.

◆

They hadn't gotten down to the open channel yet when Elle's one ski suddenly veered out the wrong way; she fell, was lying there.

"Now what!" Gonge says. "You haven't broken your leg, have you?"

"I don't know."

He stood bent over her.

"Where does it hurt?"

Elle smiled.

He was completely at sea, both were completely at sea … and now Gonge was again standing there.

"Oh, forgive me for God's sake!" he says.

"Naturally, I forgive you."

The trout bit as if it hadn't tasted red wool in ages. Even the char was tempted, and its belly glistened like the reddest gold.

Gonge stripped off his reindeer coat, tied the opening at the bottom and put all the fish in the coat, probably fifty in all.

"But I can take a few, I too," says Elle.

" You can get up on my back, you, who have hurt your leg," Gonge laughed.

They neared the tents. Gonge stopped.

"And you forgive me?"

"Of course I forgive you."

The sky is full of all kinds of weather – it often takes a long time to become good weather; but one day it's there before you realize it.

Zare and Elle were the only ones who didn't give themselves to complete indolence. They sat and sewed on homespun jackets and soft, summer reindeer hide boots. And with daring courage Elle had tackled washing Gonge's and *hoammá* Aslak's homespun clothing and beating their reindeer coats in the snow, wringing their Sámi shoes and drying them in the sun and wind.

It was a very bold undertaking, and Gonge and *hoammá* Aslak shuffled around and felt rather shamefaced. But Elle just laughed, and she didn't stop until she had gotten their hair cut, both of them. She heated up water in the large copper kettle, got them to wash with soap and presented them each with their own brass comb; and she herself stood there and saw to it that it was thoroughly done.

And while the homespun pants and jackets were hanging out to dry, Gonge and *hoammá* Aslak went around in bare coats and pants legs, with skin against skin.

During this entire miracle Zare and Sire Andaras sat and laughed themselves crooked, and Gonge laughed too, half bashfully.

"Now we'll be as clean as angels."

Yes, finally Elle tore down the entire servants' tent, that is, Gonge had to do everything, burned up the bed of twigs and Gonge had to go down into the underbrush for new twigs. But *hoammá* Aslak had taken offense; he didn't want to become the object of ridicule to the others, as much as Elle knew it.

But Gonge seems to be in seventh heaven.

"Now I am as fine and clean as a student, one who has been in the punishment institution in Trondheim."

And who would have been able to suspect that the previously so extremely unkempt Gonge could look like this when he had been cleaned up! The smoky look in his large, prominent blue eyes had become clean; even his large mouth had gotten clean and his heavy imposing body had become more at ease. And a hidden happiness laid a gleam of transfiguration over his countenance and filled his heart. Gonge was at times tempted to give air to his feelings of arrogance, in any case face to face with *hoammá* Aslak. But the feeling of happiness was so overwhelming that his joint became tender from it – a humble feeling of gratitude embraced him. He thought he might have a need to thank God for all this; but it wasn't easy to thank God for earthly love and affection – no, it was absolutely impossible. Most correct would have been actually to ask God for forgiveness that Gonge and Elle had made love in such an earthly way.

When Gonge and *hoammá* Aslak had gone to bed, on each side of the hearth, the latter could hear Gonge chortle.

"What are you laughing at?"

"I'm laughing because I can't hear you scratching yourself."

But Gonge had to laugh because he was so very happy.

Yellow cascades begin to plunge down from the heights; the open channels in the mountain lakes are getting larger; the sky and the earth have round-the-clock sun, and the south wind goes soothingly into a human's heart. It makes the snow mild to look at, and the reindeer wave their ears because the south wind brings them comfort. And in the trees the well being is apparent too.

A flock of wild geese, high up in the sky, sails northward, with the leader at the point. Here they don't fly aimlessly – order on both sides, I must request! – Don't hit one another on the wings – a little farther back there – and there – sing out! Then it goes better.

And duck song is heard from the open channels. It is the male duck that sings the words *a-anga, a-anga* – and it is like listening to angel song. Here, down is needed to fill the star cap.

Elle intended to sew a cap for Gonge: in the summer it should have only a red cloth around it; but in the winter it should be otter skin, and the star crown full of down. Gonge has never worn an otter skin cap. He was after all from the West Plateau district, and there the outside of the cap consists of small pieces of reindeer hide. Yeah, those West Plateau people! – Elegant and speckled the colors should be; but they never understood finer embellishment.

It turned into summer one day up here too, on the mountain; it was in the middle of July. During the day, when there was strong sun, the herd went up during their resting hours to the glacier to enjoy the cool breeze from the snow and ice.

One day Sire Andaras got ready to head down to the fjord bottom to the east and pick up a couple of packsaddles full of flour and sugar and coffee and seal skins for reins and bottom material for soft summer Sámi reindeer boots.

"And don't forget needles and thread spools," Zare says.

"And don't forget hand-crocheted thin lace for me," Elle says. She wanted to sew a new cap for herself and had to have a crocheted band to edge it with. And in the inland village the girls had begun a new fashion: now the earflaps on the tight fitting cap, that went under the chin, had to be so wide that farthest down they were hidden by the chin – to make the face shorter and more beautiful. And it was Anda Marit on the church hill who had begun with it, for the reason that she was big and tall and had a long, narrow face. And now it was Anda Marit, Marit Andersen, who sewed nicest and had the knack, so there. Yes, she had also begun to wear a homespun jacket that didn't reach farther down than her knees – to look smaller. If Anda Marit had come up with this ten years ago she would have been married long ago. Anyway, when Anda Marit finally got married, it wasn't because of the earflaps or the short jacket. The reason for it was that a poor Kven boy who had become a Sámi wanted to get married. And one evening he ended up in bed with Anda Marit who was lying in the dark passage in the old, small cottage on the church hill – and, good God, how he was welcome! And there was joy among the four, now quite a bit older siblings, two brothers and two sisters, all poor and eloquent, and for reasons of economy each had their own household, just reindeer meat that only brother Juoksa needed to know where it came from did they eat in common. See, now Marit was married! And a while later Juoksa too got married. Who could think that such should happen in the eleventh hour here in this house. But the eleventh hour, which in itself is a slack time, nevertheless always contains a chance in itself. The oldest sister, Gudnel, had already gotten so old that she would have said no to Jørgensen the sheriff's deputy himself. And the elder brother had a frostbitten little finger and over the course of time had begun to limp a little. But enjoyable and eloquent he was when he stood outside the door on the church hill and opened up to his listeners. The lord is merciful; he is not so strict as to who shall have joy in life. The horse and the two cows and the sheep were a common possession, as well as the riverboat that was now over twenty years old. But shouldn't Marit have had a dowry? Piera, the oldest, hit the table honorably and smart: Marit shall have a dowry! We'll raise a calf for spring!

Yes, Elle was going to sew a cap according to Anda Marit's pattern. There will be no more to tell about the four siblings on the church hill; therefore, it was just as well to remember them here on this occasion; then they can easily sink into oblivion.

***

Elle had discovered that Gonge's and her earthly love had had consequences.

Now she didn't know either up or down; the only thing she could do for the time being was to keep silent. Perhaps she ought to have entrusted it to Gonge; but she delayed and delayed. Did she love Gonge? No, she didn't really know. But love him in a way she had to, of course, since all this had been priceless for her; that it hadn't just happened at an accidentally and regrettably weak moment. But she tried to avoid the thought that she should get married to Gonge. For her own part she perhaps didn't have so much against it if it only had come to this … but what an unbearable shame for her parents! Elle married to Gonge, she who had been the most courted in the village! And in the village down there it would bring laughter. And then the exasperating: Andi Piera, he with the big, black stallion and other property, how he would laugh vulgarly and gloat inordinately! As he had laughed and gloated inordinately when Mikkal had been found guilty. Elle was on the verge of suffocation at the thought of this, a bad nightmare that made her otherwise so beautiful and pure face distorted and hard.

No, that wouldn't happen! She would sell her life at a high cost before Andi Piera would get this neck-hold on her. She hated him; he was the only person she hated. Yeah, a little resentment she had begun to harbor also for Mikkal. You had to become tired of such a handsome, heedless rich man's child, without any backbone and ambition eventually. And he had written about getting religion. We'll see at Easter!

Then she spoke alone with Gonge, said that there had been consequences.

Gonge sat there and looked at her with a humble and confused glance. And speaking from his heart he said:

"Too bad that Mikkal is in *Troandin*! Then he could have taken it on himself and married you."

Elle really had to laugh a little, as sad as the whole thing was.

"Yeah, for naturally I will not be allowed to marry you; that would bring your parents into the grave if that were to happen. And you yourself naturally wouldn't have me either."

Elle knew very well that Gonge was saying his heart's genuine conviction.

But Gonge found it difficult otherwise to comprehend that having a child was dangerous. That sort of thing often happened with the girls in the West Plateau district in the old days, and they had truly not found it difficult to get married anyway, and even to a rich man's sons.

But in the mind's dark moments Elle walked around and thought of the woods that hide so much – the mountain lakes hide their stuff, the rivers hide their stuff.

Áldu ja Miessi
Female Reindeer With Calf

Now axe blows were heard in the woods up in that valley where citizen Sire Andaras had his herd and his dwellings last winter.

It was Andi Piera among others who late in April was cutting wood up there, had bought standing timber from the state last summer when one of the state's foresters was up here, together with the forest ranger Ville Jongo, and marked trees for cutting by people. Up here at these latitudes the state owns all the forests. Andi Piera wanted to build his own house in the village, and it would be an exception that a bachelor had his own house even before he got married, own cow barn, own stable – not considering that he had property too, otherwise. Yeah, for newlyweds otherwise usually had to be satisfied with an attic room at his or her parents for the time being, often for many years.

But there were also others up here, people who intended to float timber, and small ready-notched log cabins down to the river mouth in order to sell them at the Midsummer Market to fishermen from the fjord and to small farmers by the river down there. You see, the pine forests stopped already a few miles below the inland village here.

Others cut timber on the slopes on the north side below the village. Some also in the Helligskog far up by the watercourse that runs into the river here some 15 miles below the village, and that comes from the south and forms the border with Finland. And these two form the border river on a stretch of one hundred miles, until the river below in a long stretch of powerful rapids turns off from the border and flows peacefully northward, down into a fjord bottom forty miles below the rapids.

And most of the bachelor group had already gone out to the headlands by the coast last March. Jørgensen the sheriff's deputy too. And all reindeer Sámi had gone north.

So there were relatively few people here in the inland village now in the spring months.

Right after Easter began the lakeshore children's school; they hadn't had school since last fall. Before Easter there had been upper elementary school, the confirmation school. Earlier in the winter there had been school for children of people from the higher areas.

Olle was going to school now. He had begun a couple years ago at the first *rivgu* school here. And *rivgu* is, as said before, a Norwegian woman. Olle had spent the first day with a neighbor, Ælsa Marit, and when the school was over that day, he strolled home, he too – yeah, for he thought it was so dreadful to begin with a female teacher. The next day his father had to accompany him to school, and then the difficulty had been gotten through. *Heasta*, horse – *viessu*, house – *gussa*, cow. – Our father, you who art in heaven – *rievvu*, robbery – yes, this was almost the mother tongue!

And now Olle, when you come right down to it, had avoided getting into the second class, into *skuvla-olmmai laduja*, in "the educator's" room. And one of the teachers was usually called *skuvla-olmma*, the other one, *lukkar*, the sexton; both were Sámi from here in the village. Yes, for the educator's room was unpleasant, no afternoon sun, and there was school both morning and afternoon. And there everyone sat at the same, long, wide, arched table, with the educator himself at the one end with the rod in front of himself, and he scolded and nagged so much, and still they were so dumb and deaf, these children in the class.

And now Olle had, when the spring school began, without further ado sat among the other school children in the sexton's room, pretended that he belonged here. And the sexton had winked at this, and the other children also really wanted to have Olle here. See, it worked, that too! And the room here was large and light, only a row of desks for boys along the long wall, and one for girls along the short wall. The sexton had his table on the floor, near the bookcase. And here there was an abundance of afternoon sun.

The sexton took everything calmly. After the morning devotions he examined the children in explanation of the Catechism, in Sámi: some could rattle off the printed answer by heart – others had to get ready to read the answers from the book that lay hidden behind a pile of other books; and the sexton winked at that too. Olle neither now nor ever since was able to learn a text by heart, verbatim; either he had to cheat or try to put off the teacher with a little unabashed account. The sexton never embarked upon a closer elucidation of the printed questions and answers in the explanation; perhaps the printed explanation wasn't good enough. And the teacher began to walk back and forth on the long floor; the children sat still as mice and very happily allowed him this comfort.

On the wall were hanging maps and a chart with pictures of the metric and liter systems. And once in a while he explained to the children the maps and charts; but the children studied them mostly on their own when they, all the same, didn't have much else to do in the hour. There was also a little reader with stories, partly in Sámi and partly in Norwegian. The teacher had the children read aloud in it, the lowest began and then the sexton said: next.

But the sexton always had the respect of his school children, when the bishop or school director was up here – God knows, how they had mastered what they could – *lukkar* had in any case happily avoided all the bother.

… Up in the large attic there were some remarkable booths of notched logs, and none of the children knew what purpose they had. But they who in their time built this old, delightful schoolhouse had no doubt been in the process of building it on two floors; but when they had come halfway with the second floor, someone or other had said: not needed, and they put the roof on. Oh, how these booths were fun to play hide and seek in! And then that little window with the tiny greenish panes in the west gable!

Up on the east gable tip there was an old belfry. Olle could be proud of having, in any case, one skill ahead of the others; he could get the bell to sing out, in time and festively, as if it should have been Hamas Piera himself, who rang the church bells. There was never any confused lurching in the rope when Olle rang; the bell immediately got a large and highborn sound, as soon as he took hold of the rope. Long before he began in school, even before he had gotten homespun pants, he had been able to achieve this masterpiece of perfection. When the other boys rang, the bell struck disturbed and with an ugly sound, and the rope lurched fluttery, now, for Olle it was actually difficult to see and hear such.

… Andijn, *Hooká nieida*, Hooch's daughter, substitutes in the children's school for the teacher who has gotten sick. In the breaks she always takes a tour out to the riverbank where Halle Johanas is busy building a house, which along with some timber and boards will be floated down to the river mouth as soon as the ice has broken up. The fair, slender Halle Johanas is sunburned – and can he notch! There is the sound of spring in the air; it smells of lovely raw earth, and the snow masses are melting, shining bluish in the sun and south wind.

And also in the afternoon Andijn comes walking up the riverbank and right up to Halle Johanas.

One day there are long hollows in the grounds on the village headland, and as everyone walks in the same direction, full of ponds; people are making bridges. Yellow cascades plunge down the forest hills. Andijn sits on a piece of timber and looks at Halle Johanas who is hewing a new log. People are speaking a little ways away; there's a light blue spring ring in their voices; and Olle has already made a willow flute, and the tone in it too is light blue. The pools are getting larger; yellow brown jets of water force their way down from the riverbanks. Andijn has been far up, and she comes back with pussy willows in her hand, walks into the half done log cabin where Halle Johanas is working. She tickles his bare chest with the pussy willows; her face blushes, and she laughs with a delicate sound in her voice – it smells of resin. Johanas is so silent, and Andijn gets wilder in her game, doesn't laugh any more.

***

But one morning the children's school got a message that Andijn wasn't able to come.

Halle Johanas hewed and was on the lookout for her. Had she gotten sick?

✦

The mail had come yesterday afternoon, and in the letter from the town to the east it stood that Einar Asper had come back again and had again taken up his lawyer's work; as far as one understood, nothing was wrong with him.

At the moment it had been almost unimportant to Andijn; hadn't she perhaps earlier almost had to laugh at herself when she thought of what she had said at an intense moment: I shall care for him, I shall be faithful to him, I shall be good to him, poor boy! Yes, there had been days when she didn't even remember that he existed. There had been hours when she glorified herself for being fortunate – had avoided, with the help of fate, being married to a man in whose family there had been notorious mental illness and who himself had a tumor on his brain.

But there had been other hours and days. She had had to implore God to be spared from having to be confronted by them any more.

And Andijn yesterday evening had sat quite calmly, certainly happy that such things did not affect her any more, quite certainly. And just on this occasion she had wanted to refresh herself at the thought of the adventure she was on the way to beginning with Halle Johanas. The letter from the magistrate she had read through only quite hastily – and in honest indifference.

102

But everything had been like the calm before the first thunderclap – a lightning glimpse of an image – Signe André – and it began to thunder in her mind. In a jiffy she was jerked back in time, to last fall, when a merciful intervention of fate spared her from standing face to face with what was the one terrible thing, the one unbearable thing in this world. It was in vain to examine whether it was the lightning glimpse of the image that paralyzed her mind, or whether it was the loss of that love that once, before the bad days came, had sung the one, the one song into her heart.

◆

In this spring night's bright silence it continued to thunder and lightning in her mind; in helpless anguish she sits up in bed. Lord, what evil have I done that I have been placed in this distress! No matter to be in such distress for those who can tell the other one about it. But God help the one who cannot tell it to the other one; the distances bar, the uncertainty piles up and clouds over one. And all evil visions and thoughts bind the mind, press the poison into the blood, poison, poison. Einar Asper had been full of lies and despicable evil; everything had been calculated ahead of time: report his imminent arrival, set off and then stop halfway, turn back … And down there, at many miles' distance he had reveled in the thought of how Andijn might carry on up here: wander aimlessly in an exceedingly happy expectation, for little by little, from hour to hour, to be shrouded in a suffocating uncertainty … Together with Signe André he had thought this all out; there was no bottom to her vindictive blood thirst; no, they hadn't the means to renounce this evil deed. Andijn felt bad in her hands, and her fingers tingled so stinging … A light pours in; she wants to get up already in the first morning hour, and right away she throws on a little clothing and knocks on the door to her parents' bedroom.

"But what in the world! Are you already up!" says her mother.

"Yes, for I want to leave, as soon as it is morning."

"Where?" And her mother looks half alarmed at her.

Her father rubs his drowsy eyes.

"What is she saying?"

"She says she wants to leave."

"Leave?"

"Yes, I want to go to grandfather and grandmother."

Hooch looked at the clock.

"Don't you know that it isn't more than five o'clock yet? Go to bed, Andijn."

And now Hooch has woken up.

"But I don't want to sleep any more – I want to pack up."

Her father is about to get angry, but noticed Andijn's exhausted, feverish face.

"Dear child, you must know that at this time of year it is almost impossible to get there."

"But when I go over the plateau …"

"Oh, spare us from this talk, Andijn! You know yourself how impossible it is … you can travel with one of the rafts – when the ice has broken up."

Andijn says quietly and dejected:

"But it'll be so long before that."

•

No, she couldn't manage to go up to Halle Johanas this day – she stayed inside; she was able to do that since in the morning she had confided to her mother that evil had again come over her.

Hooch went around the whole day and tried to think up something calming he could report to Andijn. Before Christmas, that dismal day it had occurred spontaneously to him that Einar had a tumor on the brain. Now it wouldn't come again, and he had to say to himself finally: in the long run one cannot think up such.

•

The next day Andijn goes out along the riverbank. Halle Johanas wasn't by the half finished house. Maybe he was home eating.

Andijn sits down on the log. The sun is hot, and the river has risen terribly these couple of days, and large open channels have developed along the shores; the ice out there has become blue-black and went like a bridge down the river ridge. There were shed reindeer antlers on it, after the reindeer herds that had passed here earlier this spring on the migration northward. And the sled tracks now lay there raised on the ice.

In the sand fall below the high riverbank, a little further up, lay a horse cadaver, half buried beneath trash and garbage – flayed – the cadaver from the horse Andijn and Halle Johanas had run into the ground during the sleigh ride Christmas day. Andijn was disgusted by the sight of it; but she couldn't refrain from looking at it. And she couldn't refrain from remembering that it was she herself who was at fault for the horse having been run into the ground; the speed had soothed her burning mind, and Johanas had not been able to refuse. Again and again she had said: faster – faster – as if she was fleeing from the memory of the burning days, when she was walking around waiting for Einar.

Halle Johanas comes, sees Andijn sitting on a log. And he is immediately clear that his plan is disrupted … Now, missed is missed; what could have happened the one time can as a rule not be made up – no, never, never! But if it comes, then it comes as a gift from heaven, without our asking for it.

Andijn says:

"I'm going north with you, on your raft. When will the ice break up, do you think?"

"It could happen at any time, if this weather continues."

"In how many days?"

"Oh, in eight days."

"Oh, good God, will it be so long!"

And Andijn stands looking sort of lost on the ice.

A flock of ducks comes like a sharp rustling from the sky and lands in the open channel. And as if appearing out of the ground, Olle is there with his old muzzle-loading rifle, fires a shot, a duck is immediately lying on the running water in the open channel; a bunch of boys from the school yard come running; a boat is shoved down the riverbank. A little while later Olle comes, surrounded by the boys, carrying the duck.

♦

But the next morning the day is buried in a sharp, biting wind from the north and under a snow-gray sky, an icy crust has formed on the pools. No sound of spring in the air; people have put on their reindeer coats. Yeah, God knows, how long this will last! Now Gudrun Gjukisdottir rides at the head of spring's death train. Travel fever has possessed Andijn; she thinks she has already become alien here – one is not where one should have been – oh, good God, how she has become alien here!

There was a despondency of biting northern wind these days. Then the sky opened again one morning.

… At noontime the blue black ice bridge in the middle of the river had broken off in a couple of places.

During the evening people were standing in groups out on the riverbank – the large ice floe on the upper side of the three-sided village headland slowly moved downward, and lay crosswise on the sharp curve at the tip of the headland, as it pushed whitening packs of ice up the hill onto the other side; and packs of splintering ice needles also rolled up onto the wall of sand below the riverbank on this side.

Here stood also Andijn and Hooch and Mrs. Lisken, and the minister's and sheriff's families.

The water was boiling between the struggling ice floes, and the flood was climbing so the eye can see it. New, large ice floes come sailing down the open water far up, and collide with the upturned masses of ice in front of the huge floe that has gotten stuck here on the curve; it roars crushing and splintering. New, white packs of ice are conjured up, and now the cascading is boiling; the torrent is rising, and over on the other side large ice floes are sailing upward, across the headland. Over the willow bushes only the tops of which can be seen now. The flocks of ducks singing at full throat above, *a-anga, a-anga*, as if in a joyful ecstasy above this great deliverance – and as a radiant conviction that none of you humans can reach us. The hay stack poles over there now barely stick up from the water; and here under the otherwise so high riverbank there are only two to three ells left down to the white pack ice.

The incessant inflow of new ice masses from above pressed down. The huge floe here suddenly broke totally; everything became loose and began to drift, and it roared like a thunderstorm. Individual floes were standing with their ends in the air, others were ground into white mountains of ice needles …

Hour after hour people were standing here and watching; the sun passed the high wooded slope on the northwest side and now it is shining in the first morning hour over the village and on the people here. The ducks are singing on the lake, and the song thrushes are singing in the birch forests over on the other side – oh, God, how the song thrush can hold forth in such a morning hour with dawning sun! And a world of other birds and animals and humans listens to the high and beautiful exultation. A world perceives that sky and earth have become beautiful.

Out on the sailing ice floes could be seen large trees with earth black roots; also traveling there was a horse cadaver on the edge of a larger ice floe.

"Halle Johanas' horse," people said.

And Hooch heard – and Andijn and all the others heard, what Johas Juhasj said:

"But Halle Johanas never got any compensation from Hooch for that horse."

Then Halle Johanas went over to Johas Juhasj and gave him a slap on the jaw and said:

"That's none of your business."

Halle Johanas avoided looking at Andijn and Hooch and the others; he walked up the riverbank and didn't look back. But people stood and looked at the horse cadaver that was traveling on an ice floe; it had become so gloomily alive. Many thought they saw that horse trotting under the sleigh bell's noise through the village.

Towards morning there also came sailing a little log house.

The next day the drifting ice had temporarily stopped.

But the third day a new ice drift began; this time it came from the two rivers above the summer pastures up above. You could also see it on the small floes: the rivers up there were full of rapids; the ice floes didn't get over them safe and sound.

Andijn comes to Halle Johanas and asks:

"When can we leave?"

"It'll be a few days yet."

"Oh, good God, it'll be more days still … But, Johanas, I have to thank you for what you did the other day."

"Did what?"

"You chastised Johas Juhasj. But I am so ashamed and embarrassed that father didn't want to give you compensation for the horse. I had thought that perhaps he would have done it now, when he saw how you behaved towards Juhas Juhasj who had shamed him in front of people."

"If I had been in your father's place, Andijn, then I wouldn't have done it either – one doesn't let oneself be guided by others' insults."

Andijn stood and looked at him – Halle Johanas really seemed to mean what he said.

"But I must all the same be allowed to travel on your raft, Johanas."

"Yes, sure, you don't have to ask."

Andijn walked into the half-finished timber house. But Halle Johanas didn't follow – not at all because he wanted to demonstrate; but he felt really and truly that a good deal had paralyzed him since Andijn had stroked his bare chest with the pussy willows she was carrying in her hand. He stood there in his tar brown, homespun jacket and hewed in the sweat of his face.

Nieida
Girl

In the pastures women and small boys stand raking all the trash together and hauling it away with wheelbarrows. They break the manure cakes with clubs on long shafts and spread it out on the ground with rakes – it's farming, that too. Erki Lemik Issak is the only one here in the area that has a wagon, a work wagon he made himself; the iron bands around the wheels he welded together himself, which more people than he himself are proud of. And since Olle is his good neighbor, he gets to borrow the wagon to carry away the trash piles, and a little of everything else too. No, there are no roads for summer driving; what is one strictly speaking going to do with a wagon? You have the river for boat travel and packsaddle roads over the plateaus for mail delivery.

The horses are loose on the fields now; they haven't gone up yet. And the stallions are fighting over mares; and not just boys, but also grownups take sides in one stallion or other. Here the other day Olle was attacked by another, larger boy with blows and kicks, Marja Piera, when Olle's father Ville Jongo's big, red stallion, that had been bought last year in Finland, after an exciting fight with another stallion that belonged to Marja Piera's uncle, had gone off with the victory and beat up and chased the other one so thoroughly that it had to go and dart around drooping at a meek distance. Oh, so humiliating for Marja Piera and his side!

It was just not with any especially good will that Olle stood outside on the field and slaved with the manure together with a half grown sister – not that he was lazy; he was a determined person who hung in there when he was only more or less healthy; but it was a humble job for a male, this. And the boys in the other homes, where there were enough women, as a rule got out of doing dung work. His father, Ville Jongo, was in the smithy or at the carpenter shop the whole day, and Olle's older brother was doing timberwork with other grownups.

But today Ville Jongo had begun sawing a heavy log into thin planks for riverboat material. The log had been rolled up onto a high scaffold under a little hillside below the wood yard. Jongo and the hired hand were each standing on one end of the debarked log and were snapping on the saw lines with a cord smeared with coal water. Ville lifted the taut cord and let it slam down, and the black line was there. They plumbed the ends and marked the underside, turned the log and snapped the saw lines on the other side too. And then they had to saw with the long, wide saw. Ville himself stood up on the scaffold, the hired hand below; they began with the trunk end and sawed a few hand's widths in; then Ville pounded in a wedge in front of the saw, and now it was like a game to saw further.

And the board sawing was also heard out from the riverbank. There, people were otherwise busy tearing down the small log houses they had built this spring, and making rafts of them. Halle Johanas had boards and a couple dozen untrimmed timbers to take along too.

Olle and the other boys were now out on the riverbank every evening to watch and lend a hand. Halle Johanas' raft was in three layers, and it was securely bound between long, fresh birch strands with bands of twisted, small thin birches. The raft's outer edges were provided with a sort of scaffolding of lumber, but quite low, for the four-fathom long oars the raft would be steered with.

Two or three smaller rafts were joined together, after one another and with birch poles.

Some of the rafts had come all the way up from that valley where citizen Sire Andaras had had his reindeer camp last winter, and they had already stood the test in the rapids up there.

There comes a raft swinging around the headland over there on the other side. It is Andi Piera's raft. Andi Piera! The miracle who had property although he wasn't married yet, but a blockhead, for he couldn't get Elle to stay in his bedroom.

Anda Juoksa from the church hill, who was also standing here on the riverbank said:

"When a bachelor makes his home ready in the way Andi Piera has, then it's just a *gufihtar-nieida*, a netherworld girl, that will be a wife in that house."

That assertion was just something Anda Juoksa hit on to say; it by no means had its root in folk belief. But such fiendish assertions steadily sneak into people's consciousness. May the Lord damn Anda Juoksa! It was like casting a spell on Andi Piera. Everyone would later repeat Anda Juoksa's utterance; people like Anda Juoksa deserved to be hanged.

Old Amarasj-Márjá from Enare, who for some reason or other had been condemned by fate to walk at an almost sharp angle, with the round angle corner in the air, suddenly comes up the riverbank with her face down like an animal; yes, she wanted to find out whether people needed more rope. For it was Amarasj-Márjá who wound the ropes, some out of the long narrow runners on pine tree roots and some of bast in the Russian flour sacks. She was almost the only one in that job here. Every winter she came driving from Enare in Finland to this village, always stayed with Erki Lemik Issak and immediately started winding ropes from bast and root runners. And she always had her sled full of dried fish from the Enare lake. The slightest hint of heckling on the part of the small boys made her as mad as a teased lemming: oh, good grief, how that upturned face there near the ground, how it could squeal on the end of the pendulous upper body. It squealed in a broken Norwegian Sámi – her own Enare Sámi no one understood here.

And at the eleventh hour Amarasj-Márjá still got some ropes sold. Stingy to death she was and had her Sámi reindeer boots full of silver coins.

All sacks and food bags were brought aboard the boats. Juhas Juhasj also had a cow on board his raft, dowry for a daughter who had been married to a man down there last winter.

And on board Halle Johanas' raft was Andijn – also Hooch and his wife; they wanted to follow their daughter a ways down. There were no fewer than five or six rafts that were now shoved out from the shore and drifted around the headland. Wives and girls and others stood on the riverbank both up here and down there, and shouted:

"Travel in good health!"

Once more a big moment! And on board *jugástat*, a dram, was drunk in departure. There were always some who wanted to follow along a ways. The flood was gloriously large, and the current twice as large as during normal water levels in the summer.

A couple headlands down Hooch and his wife and the others were rowed ashore, while the rafts continued their undisturbed drift downward.

Andijn stood on the raft and waved; and now somehow she felt ungracious in this: to be carried on a log raft downward by an overpowering flood.

Those who had rowed the guests ashore came rowing behind.

Halle Johanas kindled a fire on the raft, on a piece of grass turf he had taken along for this purpose, hung the coffee kettle over it and asked Andijn to watch it – he and a friend as a rule each had to stand on his end of the long raft and maneuver it with the long wooden oars so the raft followed in the middle of the current.

Some of the rafts are not much farther from each other than that the people can call to each other.

They rounded one headland after another. All sandbanks and outlying fields in the lower and flatter areas on the headlands had disappeared under the flood; flocks of ducks were swimming between willow and birch bushes in there. It is already nearly midnight. It is dead calm – the pine slopes on the south side are anointed with sun reflections in golden and light green, and flourishes of current eddies testify to comfort for Andijn's mind, that the otherwise so calm river is now powerfully carrying, and shore and forest that come and stay behind, testify to it. Sounds like a song thrush are hurled out too this morning of jubilation, die away in what becomes distant, and in what approaches new sounds well forth and fill the valley this sunlit night.

+

Ten miles or so below the village the river here adjoined a river that came from the south and up there formed the border to Finland.

And now it was like drifting down a flood.

"There's *Suopma*," Halle Johanas says to Andijn.

"Yes, I know, I have traveled here so many times in winter."

But so strangely barren it was on the south side here, on the Finnish side. The mountain that was absolutely high enough to be a mountain here, climbed steeply up from the flat strips of land between the river and the foot of the mountain.

And now too the pine forests began to disappear, mostly on the Finnish side, on the southwest side.

A little settlement of a couple small farms could be seen here and there, but initially on the Finnish side. Six miles below the river junction began the small, isolated settlements also on the Norwegian side.

At *Borjjasnjárga*, Sail Headland, a district on the Norwegian side, began a few smaller rapids: Andijn felt it like an elevating refreshment; the waves washed a little in over the raft. A soft shudder gives the raft speed down along such rapids.

"*Vuovdaguoika* (Outakoski) on the Finnish side there," says Halle Johanas – "with the new folk high school building you see there."

"Yes, I have been there too," Andijn says.

In the morning they passed a little, sheltered place, *Suolu*, Holmen, on the Norwegian side – 39 miles below the inland village. And now the river began to go almost straight, and with an even current. It began to blow, and it got cloudy and cold. The mountains had now become higher and more barren on the Norwegian side too. Everything had suddenly become sort of desolate and gloomy. On the Finnish side a steep and reindeer moss-rich mountain came almost down to the river.

Andijn is seized with despondency, settles down on some sacks, pulls a blanket over herself, but is freezing. The world has again gotten desolate and gloomy. Andijn weeps, tired and sleepy as she is, it is difficult to gather her thoughts. In a way everything is indifferent to her now, in a sense everything her thoughts touch is sad. Andijn fell asleep, and Halle Johanas came and threw some more covers over her.

It began to storm, and the rafts had to come alongside land so as not to risk being driven into a very poorly situated beach.

It calmed down later in the afternoon, and the rafts were maneuvered out into the middle of the current.

In the evening, fifty miles below the inland village, the speed in the current became threatening. Halle Johanas and his friend went back and forth on the raft and tied down everything that was loose. Andijn's heart beat.

"Can't I be rowed ashore here?"

"No, it's not necessary here," shouted Halle Johanas.

An inn could be seen up on a high mountain on the northern, Norwegian side, and there to the north climbed a large *Gáisá* glacier, with sun halo around the crown of snow and ice.

Far below it boomed and banged, like a subterranean roar.

"For God's sake, put me ashore!" Andijn shrieked.

"It's too late now," Halle Johanas shouted; and Andijn herself saw that it was too late. And before she realized it the first waves poured in over the raft. She ran forward and clawed firmly into Halle Johanas' homespun jacket.

"Don't hold onto me!" He shoved her cruelly away, and maneuvered the raft with clenched teeth through the surging masses of water in these rapids that was a mile long and filled the air with a sound stifling everything. Andijn lay there and held her hands over her eyes. The masses of water surged all at once in over the raft, and each time Andijn screamed and gasped for air, like someone drowning. The stretch of rapids was full of huge boulders that rose up in low water; but now they were inundated and rolled up powerful swirls that twisted the whiteness out of them; and also the beaches were full of boulders that lay there helter-skelter. But Halle Johanas and all the others were used to traveling in such wild rapids from childhood on; at a long distance they could see the worst dangers and maneuver the raft away.

The raft then took an extra spurt, and now it became sort of smooth water again. It hadn't taken more than some few minutes to ride down along this mile-long stretch of rapids.

But the river continued to run from rapids to rapids and would continue intermittently an entire new 50 miles downward.

The valley had become narrow down here; every so often it widened out and gave room for one or another little settlement, with birch forests around.

Andijn walks forward again and says to Halle Johanas:

"Now that it is over I almost think it was fun."

"This here was just child's play; but wait until we go down the Big Chasm."

"Then you'll surely put me ashore?"

"Of course."

"But is it dangerous to be on the raft?"

"That depends. It is of course not without danger."

Andijn is silent. Then she says:

"But it would be exciting to try."

"Then you'll have to do it on your own responsibility."

The raft is swallowed by one rapid after another, and is sent on.

A few miles farther down Johas Juhasj shouts, his raft is now right in front of Halle Johanas':

"Up there in the little valley is the Otsego church. It's made of stone, and that's where Virkal preaches, the great preacher; people come from distant districts to hear him. He preaches the way Læstadius taught."

The raft hurries with the fast moving current. A little neighborhood here, another there – with miles in between.

Now a new roar is heard far down – a distant, threatening sound.

"Shall I row you ashore while there is still time?" Halle Johanas says to Andijn – "then you can stroll over a ridge; all you have to do is follow the path – all the way until you come to a farm below the Big Chasm, the last farm on the Finnish side."

116

Andijn stands thinking it over.

"I think I'll hazard it … there's no hurry to come ashore yet … I think I'll risk it."

The raft begins to hurry with greater speed; and the tumult and din down there increases. Then Andijn is suddenly seized by a helpless, terrible fear:

"Row me ashore!"

Halle Johanas blanched – it was at the very last instant. He shoves the boat over the scaffold at the raft edge.

"Jump into the boat!" And he rows ashore with all his strength.

"Jump out!" And in the next instant he rows as if possessed after the raft that he reaches when it has already shot into the first large eddies, barely gets the boat up onto the raft, but has no time to lash the rope to the raft that is hurrying forward. He throws a rope around his waist and the scaffold so as not to be washed overboard, shoves out the wooden oars, straight ahead, maneuvers … The Big Chasm is pressed in between steep rock walls and slabs of rock so sheer that Halle Johanas with his glance which is not directed so far down, dimly perceives the channel down there as a shiny lake … the underwater rocks jeer waist-high; wrathful they billow up over the masses of water; they live as white flames, but are forced together and taken away by the storm. The cow on Juhas Juhasj' raft bellows from the depths of fear, but cannot be heard; the big eyes stare forward, horror-stricken, but the animal has nothing else to do than to try to stand continually on its four strong legs and stare at this booming and boiling abyss. The raft moves pitching down, the front end is lifted up and dives under all at once.

◆

So! – and now this eternity of a few minutes was over. All the rafts, with almost one exception, drifted somewhat whole and unassailed down over a weak rapids below the Big Chasm. But one had been torn to pieces since it had come in contact with an underwater rock near the shore on the Finnish side, and Juhas Juhasj said to the people who were on the remains of it:

"It's hell that people always are tempted to maneuver too far to that side, and it is always people without experience; they are afraid that the raft in the gentle curve there will move too close to the shore on the other side. But the waters don't turn toward the shore there; they follow the curve."

Here at the Big Chasm the river left the Finnish border – or more correctly put: the border left the river and went into the mountains, first, in a southerly direction, made a turn far to the east, and didn't meet a proper river until it reached the Russian border far to the east, at Border-Jakob's river.

Here below the Big Chasm the river was a calm, inundated river, with a little, idyllic village of small farms on the riverbanks on both sides, and with a little chapel on a plain on the south side.

Only when they had come out of the Big Chasm's abyss could Halle Johanas take a glance back and discovered immediately that the boat was gone; his friend who was standing on the lower end of the raft and holding on to the maneuvering oars shouted to him that the boat had been washed overboard way up.

Down here on the quietly running torrent they stood and looked for the boat, and yes, there it came drifting down, torn up from end to end.

"What in the hell!" shouted Juhas Juhasj from his raft, "is that your boat, Halle Johanas?"

Juhas Juhasj rowed after the badly mistreated boat and dragged it to Halle Johanas' raft. Not much was said on this occasion. The Big Chasm sometimes demands a sacrifice.

But his friend swore: "Why in the hell should Halle Johanas row that damned girl ashore! – And when she didn't want to go ashore earlier then they should just have tied a rope around her and fastened it to a crossbar instead of rowing her ashore."

Halle Johanas was pale and said nothing. Then he said:

"But we don't have to tell others about it. Let it be an accident!"

The rafts put ashore below the riverbank on the north side; here people would sleep. It was morning and it had begun blowing a little; it would be difficult to maneuver the rafts in the weak current down here.

And up on the riverbank was Lemik Jouna's farm, and Lemik Jouna was a well-to-do bachelor whom everyone expected would marry the fabulously beautiful Mar'ja there on the south side. And Mar'ja wasn't just pretty, she was also good and kind and clever, and all traveling bailiffs and ministers and attorneys and similar gentlemen stayed at Mar'ja and her parents' when they were going to take a break here in this village. But Lemik made no preparations in that direction. He himself looked like a gentleman, fair and tall, had a long, narrow face; but perhaps he didn't appreciate that Mar'ja suddenly had great gentlemen as guests. But he should have just known. No, first it's so difficult to know such, and much more difficult to believe it. Faith and confidence is a noble, but sadly rare gift.

118

Lemik Jouna asked how people lived up there in the inland village.

"Well, just fine," says Juhas Juhasj, "and on a raft that is expected, there is a female prospect for you, if she doesn't perish in the Big Chasm beforehand. Row aboard and take a look at her, you! She has red embroidered gloves, and reindeer coat and jacket in the storehouse at home."

+

Now a boat arrived with Andijn on board from the Finnish side.

"I don't know how much I should thank you, Johanas, for your rowing me ashore at the last moment. I would have died of fright if I would have been on board the raft – I understand that now."

... Then Halle Johanas and his friend sat on board the raft and looked at the completely destroyed boat. They are both quite simply despondent. Now they have to rent a boat when they head up again; they have to take along some goods home with themselves when they come from the Midsummer Market by the river mouth.

"And last winter you lost your horse, Johanas," his friend says, "and that was also Andijn's fault."

"Let us clearly not talk about this now," says Halle Johanas. But he couldn't take his eyes off the destroyed boat – one of Ville Jongo's masterpieces that Halle Johanas had bought last year for 40 kroner. Forty kroner doesn't grow on trees within the country. And that boat he of course could have had for many a long year – and the horse he could also have had for many a long year. The boat was of the new river boat type that Ville Jongo had created some ten years ago and had gotten a medal for at the exhibition in Tromsø. It was five fathoms long, the width no greater than one and a half ells at the widest in front, where the wide gunwales were joined with a thicker piece of wood that had not been bent with force, but cut after insertion; that made the front end stronger, and in that piece there was also a natural section for the oarlocks. The high prow was extended forward and had a slightly inward bent and cut-out bow grip of a hand's width running lengthwise. The front end was a little wider at the top, so the boat was lifted up when, during poling up the rapids, it was pushed into a plunge-step. The sternpost was lower.

No, Halle Johanas couldn't take his eyes from the boat. Now he looked at it because it was destroyed. Before, many a time, he had stood and looked at it, because all of its remarkably beautiful lines could make his mouth water. It was tarred and still shone so reddish light brown.

The raft people who almost hadn't slept during this trip slept the entire day.

It calmed down toward evening, and the rafts maneuvered out into the current again. Only now did Andijn discover that Halle Johanas' boat had been damaged during the trip down the Big Chasm, and she was very distressed about that. But she had no idea that she was to blame for it. And Halle Johanas kept quiet about it. But his friend couldn't restrain himself any longer – he said:

"Johanas didn't have time to fasten the boat to the raft when he came rowing back; he should have put you ashore earlier."

A shadow slipped over Andijn's face.

"Then I will pay for the boat."

"That is just damn nonsense he's talking, him there!" said Halle Johanas, his voice trembling.

"I want to know whether it is my fault?"

"It is not your fault, and let us not talk about it any more."

And Andijn was silent – and she bore in mind that she had been at fault in the horse's death last winter, and that her father had not wanted to compensate for it. It felt so vague and icy in her mind, for a long, long time … she froze, she got hot, and she froze again … until little by little she was swept along by it, as if she were in a fever: the thought that she had no idea about, what she was drifting towards. Should she go to the town to the east where Einar Asper was, or should she continue down to the river mouth where the magistrate was, and where she also had her aunt? Oh, God, to be able to travel far, far away, with a ship! But look, one can't do that, and the world out there doesn't give weight to ones sorrows; they are just bait for the hard, hard world.

◆

A good ways below the Big Chasm the flooded river turned to the north. About ten miles below, it passed another small rapids, the last one. And here the first royal road in these parts went over a low, ten-mile-wide isthmus on the east side and continued farther to the east, along the north side of the long fjord to a couple towns and other fishing stations to the east.

On the riverbank and right at the end of the royal road stood young, happy Jao Jao, a half Kven, who had recently started a little business in a storeroom called by him "The Mustard Seed."

"How's it going with 'The Mustard Seed,' Jao Jao?" shouted Juhas Juhasj!

"Excellent, Juhas Juhasj! I have to begin very soon making my shop larger, but I don't plan to start eating and drinking, and then the Lord will keep me from dying tomorrow."

"Yes, wise is that man who plants mustard seeds at the end of a new royal road."

The birch woods on the hills on both sides began to get a bit poorly to look at. The river got wider; and far to the north you could already see the blue, bare mountains on both sides of the river mouth.

Andijn comes running to the front of the raft, to Halle Johanas.

"Put me ashore, Johanas! I want to go to the town."

"But we don't have any usable boat here now; you should have said it earlier, then we could have called to Jao Jao and asked him to come fetch you."

Andijn is silent. Then she says:

"Well, that's fine that in a way it's too late. I would rather go down to the river mouth, to my aunt after all."

And Andijn walks back.

✦

The distance between the steep, sheer mountains on both sides of the river mouth is large; the huge sandbanks are now inundated by the river with broad, entirely flat moors with birch forest and one or another little farm on both sides. The mountain on the west side is a single rock-strewn slope. The one on the east side shines with red sandstone and red violet waves of sand, now in the summer night's sun.

The fjord appears blue to the north, between barren, steep mountains.

Čáppa dálki
Fair Weather

Juhas Juhasj, Halle Johanas and a few others had set up their ready built log cabins on the beaches, on the east side, below the hill at the market place and church and parsonage and doctor's residence and the new clerk's residence.

A little further up was Elnagården – named after the long dead petty king in this district, Rudolph Greiner's beloved and grandiose wife Elna. Rudolph and Elna Greiner's burial ground was an attraction here. Greiner had owned several fishing stations and businesses out along the fjord, had had a large commercial center at Jarholmen farther down. There was just a very small reef of rock near the beach on the west side of the mouth of the fjord; but it was so easy to come alongside that small island with the ferry from the steamship stopping place there on the east side, just below the large sandbanks in the river mouth. But it was only at high tide that the ferry could come through the channels in the last sandbanks in the river; at ebb tide these formed a whole sandy desert, on whose banks lay hundreds of seals sunning themselves after the fishing journeys at sea and up to the salmon fences in the river.

The dear departed Greiner had also had stores further up, and he had been able to serve liquor everywhere.

His son, who was also named Rudolph, ran the store on Jarholmen and also had a fishing business at a fishing station on the west side of the fjord, far out. And this Rudolph Greiner was married to Andijn's aunt, born Hooch, from the city on the fjord to the southeast, but the petty king in the sense his father had been, he was not; he was though a solid and hard-working, honest man, in every respect looked after the village's and district's well being and was its natural mayor.

But the abode was Elnagården, now as always.

The Midsummer Market was in full swing. Here had appeared a bunch of fishermen and others from the fjord inlets out there, from the districts in the lower part of the valley. Yes, even people from the Finnish side up there had come down here, although they didn't have permission to float timber to Norway; in return they got the timber free for their own use at home.

The market booths had been erected on the crest of the hill near the church. But the large-scale trade took place far down on Jarholmen at Rudolph Greiner's.

The sea Sámi from the fjord out there sort of kept to themselves around the market booths; centuries of turf hut life in the fjord inlets had left its mark on them. But Juhas Juhasj and his fellow villagers could say exactly where the one or the other was from. See, those there are from the fjord to the southeast; they have misunderstood us and put decorative trim on their backs too! And Juhas Juhasj laughs with open mouth. Also those from the little idyllic village right below the Big Chasm, and who, for that matter, judging from body and countenance hardly had a drop of real Sámi blood in them, are different from the slapdash people from Juhas Juhasj' village. But Juhas Juhasj, who also had a compassionate heart, really felt sorry for a couple of young boys from the fjord out there: they walked around showing off, tussled with the girls and were stupidly funny.

"Stupidly funny anyone can be," says Juhas Juhasj to Halle Johanas, "but, good God, it is sort of indecent for simple people to try to show off."

***

Andijn and her aunt, Lady Greiner, sat in a room that faced the river, at Elnagården. It was the day after Andijn arrived with the raft.

The rooms were so large here, in any case the three that faced the river. And everything that was here seemed to have been here in all eternity, for that matter not much different than at grandfather's in the town to the east. Here as at grandfather's there were so many old Russian things: silver candlesticks, copper plates on the walls in the dining room, birch bark crocks on the shelves, the pictures on the walls. Most everything was from Archangel, and mostly gifts from the red bearded skippers from Archangel, and that they had with them when they came sailing in June with their loads of flour for the Norwegian fishing stations to operate tusk trade with the fishermen and otherwise to sell part of the cargo to Norwegian businessmen. Customs and such didn't exist in this case. There was not the means to fight up here; the people had enough just getting one another bread and fish.

Her aunt had gotten out some crocheting for Andijn; she herself sat knitting a stocking.

They had sat and talked about a lot about the inland village up there; but now the conversation began to come to a halt as it were … It was a little difficult to go into …

This was in the afternoon. And Andijn wondered to herself whether magistrate Ludvig Mæhre had yet paid a visit. At home he had let it be apparent that everything between him and Andijn had already sort of been decided. The same in the letters to her this spring; although she hadn't with a single word, much less in her behavior toward him, given him any encouragement in that direction. A rare magistrate, this Ludvig Mæhre. But anyway she was sort of disappointed that he had not paid a visit today.

After a little painful silence her aunt says:

"Yes, your mother wrote to me last winter a long letter about … Yes, my child, the world is complicated. And Einar Asper couldn't help it, the poor thing. That sort of thing has happened before in his family, it is said. And then it is so easy to succumb to fear, as soon as something seems to be the matter with one."

Andijn's fingers began to shake where she sat and crocheted. Everything was at sea for her again, and she didn't know what she should say. In her helpless confusion she was on the verge of breaking into tears.

"Tell me, Andijn, from what I understood from your mother's last letter to me, then you don't care much for the magistrate."

Andijn was about to say no, she didn't; but she had a lump in her throat; she was quiet. Her aunt continued:

"And then it will hardly affect you to hear …"

Andijn awoke suddenly.

"Hear what?"

"Well … Well, it is your own fault. You didn't really want to know him after all."

"No, I didn't … Well, what did you want to say?"

Andijn sat as if on nails.

"Well, so he had to look for another – and it is your own fault."

"And who is it?"

Andijn's face seemed to ask in two stages.

"Miss Signe André."

The crocheting fell from Andijn's hands. An entire earth seemed to make a revolution right in front of her eyes.

"And I who thought …" Andijn stopped herself with all her might.

"What did you think, my child?"

"No, it makes no difference."

Andijn got up and broke into laughter.

"He's strange, this Ludvig Mæhre!"

And Andijn laughs way too much; a world has been revolving in front of her eyes. But now she becomes afraid of having exposed her heart too much. She quivers from a convulsive attempt to put a damper on herself.

"Yes, I am going to really congratulate the magistrate when I meet him," she says. "And I basically think he is an excellent person when you get down to it. A little sly and mechanical of course – and he is so busy asserting himself. But certainly an excellent person, as said."

"But is she here then?"

"No, not now. She has to take care of her telegraph in town. But she was here just after the ice breakup was over, and he followed her back. And I hear that they are old acquaintances from the capital."

Little by little Andijn was seized by second thoughts; and unbeknownst to herself she sat quite taciturn.

Her aunt says:

"So there can't have been much to it anyway, what people have talked about … yes, that there was something between Miss André and Asper, that poor Asper. And it's too bad with that man: walk around with that dread in him. Well, it is said that he was operated on for a brain tumor when he was in the capital. But one doesn't actually know much about it."

Andijn couldn't help it that her heart again knotted up.

"But you can at any rate thank your God, my child, that he himself discovered the danger in time; and that danger will always be there. You have your life before you; you are no more than nineteen years yet."

***

Miss Signe André had come to the town by the fjord to the southeast at the beginning of November last fall, a little before attorney Einar Asper made his halfway trip to the inland village to celebrate his wedding to Andijn Hooch. She had come as a telegrapher. It soon became clear to everyone that she and Asper were acquainted from Oslo. Asper had immediately taken her to lawyer Toddy-Jakobsen's family. She became a friend of the family.

But Asper had thus turned around when he had come only halfway to the inland village. And with the first ship, fourteen days later, he had traveled to the capital to be operated on, as he himself said.

In the little town by the fjord the few cultured people were immediately clear that Signe André wasn't an ordinary telegrapher. But she was almost unable to ramble about outside the Toddy-Jakobsen family. Well, you couldn't care less about that in itself, as the merchant Akra said. But Signe André was Signe André: she was really tiny and slender; but God what a posture, what a gait. And her big, strong blue eyes could not be frightened, although it was granted that she always seemed to be sort of on the watch – for what? Well, for everyone, perhaps mostly for herself. But when she smiled, and her two front teeth stepped forth in her pure mouth, see, then women were themselves ready to smile a little again in self-denying admiration. It was sort of like a little of a higher world had opened up for them in this smile in this face that was so pure in form and expression. She smiled with the corners of her mouth pulled a little inward so that her lips were puckered. Her nose went almost straight down from her forehead, a sober, common straight nose, a little high. And just as pure in posture was her firmly built but slightly slender body.

… Now, Norway was long, and during midwinter the coastal ships came up here to this country's most distant town only once a month. But nevertheless, gradually one got small glimpses into Signe André's situation: one fine day the entire town knew that her father, a former lawyer, lived like a drunken bum in the capital, was probably of good family, to be sure in a more modest sense. And this man, when the students one evening had dragged him along for fun to an informal party at the Student Society, was supposed to declaim large portions of the *Iliad* in Greek. And the rumors around this man simply formed kaleidoscopically, according to whether people were in the mood when the talk was about Signe André. And when didn't one talk in this little, reclusive fishing town about Signe André?

Now, God only knows, it wasn't to hide away or hunt for a place where she could be, so to speak, incognito, that she had come up here as a telegrapher. But that's her business for what reasons she had sought to come up here. And incidentally: the first concrete proof that people had found out who her father was, she got one day when a boy came with a telegram to send off – to lawyer André, Vaterlandsbroen, Oslo. Collect 80 øre from Pancake, borrowed from me last year. Doffen.

She took the telegram without blinking and sent it. It wasn't composed by just anybody, no, but by a woman and a gentlemen, and neither of these had a tumor on the brain.

But one shocking and impossible nut people had to crack above all, and that they were unable to crack: Signe André's eternally constant goodness towards Einar Asper, the tall, thin attorney with the dark eyes, once Andijn Hooch's fiancé. She was together with him that day last fall when Asper headed to the interior – she was with him that day he turned back – and that day he traveled south "to be operated on" – and that day early this spring when he came back. And even now when there obviously was something developing between her and magistrate Ludvig Mæhre over there at the river mouth. Even though it was notorious that Asper and Mæhre couldn't stand each other. Asper had his own nonchalant way of being sarcastic to the poor, struggling Ludvig Mæhre. People knew that Asper and Mæhre and Signe André were old acquaintances from Oslo. So, a sort of poetry of the distances, if you will.

◆

Much of all of this Mrs. Greiner in Elnagården could tell her niece Andijn.

Andijn almost had to grab herself by the arm. Was this everything? Signe André who was tied to the very worst in Andijn's world; she was accordingly not guilty, when all was said and done. A literal emptiness prevailed in Andijn's mind for the moment. She was like a captive of punishment who after a lengthy prison stay suddenly finds herself under God's free heaven, in the freedom she had so long dreamt of … So what? Is this all? But when she had collected herself Andijn knew that this feeling of emptiness in her was hiding something in her that somehow caused her thoughts to stop for a moment: what did she have to do when she again stood face to face with Einar? … He who in the last half year had become so infinitely far away from her and at the same time deceived her so unpleasantly near that she involuntarily had been driven to hear Asper and not Einar in her heart. An overwhelming feeling of rebellion rose up in her: he who had caused her all this … never! But when she had somehow refreshed her mind in this rebellion sufficiently, she again got air under her wings and in her lungs to be able to get a new twinkle that gave her thoughts a new speed: a prospect had been opened up for her. She could eye the goal during the flash of passion: when she had him beneath her feet … For at the point of exhaustion to again linger on a refreshing thought that everything became good again … Einar, my poor boy. And if you succumb to what you fear, then I shall be good to you, care for you, sing that hymn to you that you said last year always made you brighter in your mind.

***

But now a letter came to Andijn and Mrs. Greiner from the town with a special messenger.

Fridtjof Hooch, Andijn's brother, had come home from Archangel – blind; both eyeballs had been taken out. He was now with his grandparents in the town. How this accident had happened, there was unfortunately neither opportunity nor time to tell. But Andijn had to come immediately, and Mrs. Greiner would get a more detailed account of it later. Fridtjof was otherwise healthy and cheerful and seemingly almost unaffected by the ill fortune – incomprehensible enough – if not to say unpleasant enough, for yesterday evening he still sat and laughed and told anecdotes.

… Mrs. Greiner sat and held Andijn by the hand; but Andijn didn't cry. She moaned a little sobbingly every so often, without tears.

Some have stores in them, others not, when life robs most of all.

"I must have a boat ride up to the royal road, aunt."

And now she remembered what she had forgotten in these unsettled days: Halle Johanas had been without a boat. She found him down at the market place.

"Buy a new boat, Johanas. Here is the money. And then you and your friend can give me a ride up to the royal road, to *Jáguidgieddi.*"

"I've already rented a boat. And we're just starting to begin poling upstream; we have shopped and everything is already in the boat."

It was 18 miles up to *Jáguidgieddi.*

***

Andijn sits in a gig and rides over the low, ten-mile-wide isthmus between the river and the fjord bottom to the east. Small tarns here and there, with star grass around, a little underbrush of birch and willow, and along the road went the telegraph line and a fence that was pretentiously announced as a national fence, set up with the aim of preventing the fifteen to twenty thousand reindeer that the Sámi had here in the east from running free without herding on summer pasture on the very large, spacious peninsula to the northeast, and from turning back before the statutory time in the fall.

•

Andijn suddenly became aware that she had become a grown-up human in the course of this day: the young mind felt so strong, the brain thought clearly. Never could she have imagined that she would be able to take that message in this way. Even the thought of Einar Asper and the – of course unavoidable – imminent meeting with him was clear and grasped, and almost mild.

The road began to steepen, and now she saw the fjord and Heemskerk farmstead, a large, stately building with side wings and vaulted roof like a trunk lid. Andijn was slightly related to the Heemskerk family, also to the Knack family far out at the national border on the south side of the mouth of the fjord. The Hooch, Heemskerk and Knack families had for roughly two centuries formed the petty king dynasties up here in these parts; but this had gradually ebbed with them. New people had begun to lift their heads. Of the Heemskerk family here at the fjord bottom there wasn't much more left than the fabulously high, crooked noses. Otherwise, the three families were also tied to each other through marriages at earlier times.

◆

During the night Andijn came to the large inn and woke the family. And already in the morning she was on the local ship that was outward-bound. She who came from the inland, in spite of everything else that now occupied her, could not refrain from looking at the turf huts and the small cabins along the barren shores, and at the many lame Sámi who showed up at the small ports of call on both sides of the fjord, and at the curious, poorly placed yellow, red and blue cloth trim on the coat backs. "They have misunderstood us," as Juhas Juhasj said. The plain wooden church on the north side of the fjord seemed like a cathedral in the middle of all this meager development of human abodes. Andijn had traveled here often enough; but always these naked landscapes and cabins squeezed together and people were just as strange to her; the small Nordland's boats on the banks of the seashore though seemed to give these people's homes a little more comforting touch.

Andijn sits on deck; here, fortunately, there were no passengers on board whom she knew personally. And just as she is busy with the thought of her brother she is again in a confused whirl of the ever false: how should she behave toward Einar ... and now it is just Einar, not Asper ... until she suddenly says to herself that she will say Asper to him, not Einar ... She could perhaps say Einar too, but then she would immediately correct it and say Asper.

Then she is occupied with the vision in her heart: her brother, Fridtjof, with the empty eyes, blind, will never again see any light and life ... Who had not been struck by the bristlingly healthy and beautiful abundance in Fridtjof's blue eyes; in stature he was the pure athlete to look at, and he always walked like a steel spring.

And yet there is just now a thought that causes Andijn to be startled ... he is perhaps at fault in the whole misfortune.

132

Andijn, to be sure, had understood from her parents last winter that there was something the matter with Fridtjof – well, she had understood that he drank. The few and almost insignificant lines he had sent his sister every so often, and really just out of politeness, contained nothing that would indicate that he was in a bad way.

… No, any explanation for it she could nevertheless not give herself. Fridtjof was of course so extremely honest in his temperament, never suspicious, always so taken up with wanting to understand others. The only slightly frightening thing with him was that he could laugh so bleakly, almost weirdly unpleasant, when something really had shocked him. But a penchant for drink he had never had, as far as Andijn understood. Well, once he had gotten drunk – not drunk, rather dead drunk; but then he was just an inexperienced boy of 12 or 13 years … Poor father and mother when they get to hear this … But it might also be – and perhaps this was the most likely – that infatuation was involved. Fridtjof probably had great influence on women and was surrounded. But he always took that sort of thing so solemnly; he had no sense for this half jovial flirting.

Halle Johanas had promised to pole straight home, so Andijn's letter would reach her parents long before the mail which in the summer had to go around the entire coast up here, and then with mail carriers in over the plateau on the west side of the inland village – and just this stretch was all of 110 miles.

The local ship crosses the fjord. The cod fishing is long since past: but the drying racks for fish at the small stopping points are full. The fishing boats that are now seen out on the fjord are fishing for pollack. A Russian flour cargo boat lies at anchor at a somewhat larger place on the north side.

Not until three o'clock did the boat near the town, and still they were only half way to the large mouth of the fjord to the east. As usual with the towns up north, this one, to look at from the sea side, was mostly just a complex of tall, brownish yellow storehouses on posts in the sea covered with greenery. Well, and then the church highest up on the hill, and a bunch of yellow and blue painted Kven houses. But behind the storehouses was the town – most of what counted – around a larger town square.

A couple of Russian cargo boats from Archangel lay in the harbor. It was probably with one of them Fridtjof had come. Otherwise, the harbor was empty of the small vessels that it was otherwise usually full of; the vessels were now sealing on the ice in the Arctic Ocean.

The ferrymen came rowing out to the local ship; the harbor was too shallow for steamships.

***

Andijn couldn't avoid catching a glimpse of Einar – yes, at this moment he was again Einar – before she climbed up over the high stairway with rungs on the side and with an elegant iron railing on the outside. It would perhaps have been easier if she hadn't seen him just now; but anyway – anyway it was a relief. She walked hesitantly up the steps – not out of fear of meeting her brother with the empty eyes, but that Einar would have time to recognize her, in case he should happen to look back …

***

Andijn met her grandmother in the hallway. Her grandmother opened the door to the corner room; she didn't come in right away. Fridtjof sat alone in there by the window; he had a dark blue pince-nez in front of his empty eyes, but looked toward the one entering. When Andijn wasn't able to make a sound right away, Fridtjof said with a calm voice:

"I hear that it is your steps, Andijn."

Andijn fell around his neck and cried, cried, cried. He tolerated this patiently, then freed himself gently from her arms.

"I'm not unhappy, Andijn. Sit down on that chair there. … Yeah, good grief, I know so very well that this is terrible for you. And naturally you think that I am just trying to make myself courageous. But you will very soon learn to understand that it's not just idle talk from me when I say that I am not unhappy. And when all is said and done then that's what it's a question of – whether one is happy or unhappy."

"I've sent a letter with Halle Johanas; he was going to pole straight up, and then father and mother will be able to be here already by the beginning of next week."

"I wrote to father and mother before I left Archangel, and told them what I have told you now. … Now they will naturally come down here anyway; there's nothing to be done about that. You are probably hungry now; but we are going to eat dinner soon. … And how are you, Andijn?"

"I?"

"Yes."

"Thanks, I'm fine, Fridtjof."

"Well, mother wrote to me last winter about that, you know, but you shouldn't give a damn about that, Andijn. You aren't even really grown up yet. And there isn't anything irretrievable in such. – No, this is not irretrievable."

134

And now Fridtjof smiled his little smile.

"And then you'll naturally soon tackle it again. Well, I'm kidding maybe a little maliciously. But let me say right away: you perhaps don't know how this has happened to me. I myself do not want to tell you that, on the whole not go into that, in front of you. But you will hear it from grandmother; I've had skipper Gregorij tell grandfather and grandmother the whole thing."

***

But skipper Gregorij had only been able to relate the external incident.

Which sounded thus:

Already last fall Fridtjof had gotten onto the slippery slope of vodka. And then that day had come after Russian Easter. Fridtjof is sitting together with an older woman in a little restaurant, Morskoi Restaurant. He is not drunk; his glass stands empty. The older woman is a lady; but the lady is in a greasy, black dress and has a large, black veil on her hat. She is not in mourning; she has always gone like this; people were used to seeing her sit in a corner at Morskoi Restaurant in this black, greasy dress, and with a veil on her hat.

"So, they have that evening when you don't drink any wine; she had a glass of cheap wine in front of herself."

"Yeah," said Fridtjof, "and she said nothing more. The lady puts a pince-nez on her nose and reads a little in the evening newspaper."

"I don't think I can manage any more," says Hooch – he looks in another direction.

"One is not obliged to explain what one cannot manage. One has the duty to take account of ones own weakness," she says coldly, unmoved. She reads a long time in her newspaper, and Fridtjof sits quietly and silent.

"Don't I look like a bear?" he says.

"Yes."

And she continues to read. Fridtjof gets up.

"Are you going?" She sees that he feels for something in his pocket. "You are nervous, I see."

"Yes, I wonder whether I shouldn't take a glass of wine."

"When you don't know, when you can't drink a glass of wine with good conscience, then you ought not to do it."

Fridtjof sits down. Sits quietly.

"But we can't live either with a good conscience, and yet we have to live."

"Hm."

Fridtjof gets up again.

"No, I still do not want to have wine." He extended his hand to say goodbye, and before he had even gotten out of the door, the older woman sat in the black, greasy dress, pince-nez on her nose, and continued to read in her newspaper — and she also looked like someone who has rescinded the difference between life and death.

… The constable had to take a closer look for the man who walked into the entranceway there; and he hit the man on the elbow as soon as the man pulled the trigger. And the man was brought to the hospital.

That was all the skipper had been able to tell Fridtjof's grandparents about what had happened that day.

But the skipper had confided to old Hooch privately that Fridtjof often on board had talked in his sleep about something he saw in a mirror.

… Eight weeks had passed now since Fridtjof's accident. He doesn't have pain any longer, but when he is lying in bed at night, before he has fallen asleep, a twinge can go through his body — which is still happening — and then he sees a red flash before the eyes he no longer has. Now, there is nothing remarkable in that: someone who has had a leg amputated can feel pain in the toes of the foot that is gone; someone who has suddenly become deaf in one ear can hear a chorus of voices — just in the deaf ear: pleasant compliments, words of abuse, songs, all according to what ones own mind is in the mood for. Think about coffee, and the voice in the deaf ear says coffee a hundred times, if your inner hurdy-gurdy doesn't give you other words that take precedence.

"Actually, it was due to nothing other than that I accidentally was walking around with a revolver on me that evening. I had also experienced many similar dangerous feelings earlier in the course of the winter; but then I didn't have a revolver. Thousands of that kind of thing would happen if people in my mood had revolvers on themselves at the right moment. Frankly speaking, I had no reasonable basis to do it, virtually none other than that I had started to pamper myself for the revolver that day."

No, Fridtjof Hooch doesn't shudder at the thought that he had lost his vision forever.

But during the night he relives that evening in Archangel, when he came barging into the living room of his host, merchant Wasilij, and with his cane hit a large wall mirror, went into the dining room where the family was sitting and eating. And there he grabbed the tablecloth and jerked the whole table setting down onto the floor, so glasses and cups and plates veritably sang in this clattering abomination of destruction ... see, then Fridtjof knows that blood went to his head ... the mirror, the mirror ... a mirror that is placed at an angle in a corner gapes into the side room: it is the devil's tree of knowledge. He who wants to make you a troll, will let you see it in the mirror ... a hallucination at the entrance to the world of twilight and nightmare. Irma, this was your joy and your pleasure on earth! Now, good grief, you thought perhaps that I was going to come barging into you and him, and make a scandal; for such was your poor soul's only joy and pleasure. But I didn't come. You knew and understood what I had seen; but I didn't come. And you were immediately ready to ignore your partner – to collect me for the next crossroads – for the next surprise in the mirror. Your red-haired stamina didn't betray you, and I was a fool that let myself be blinded yet again; and yet again you got yourself to stand face to face with your surprise in the mirror. To be sure, I loved you – and, to be sure, I had long suspected that that kind of surprise procured your only joy and pleasure; but I could nevertheless sort of not believe it. I couldn't believe that you in dead earnest committed deeds that didn't demand anything but an unpleasantly inclined mind. You loved me, and could nevertheless not refrain from doing such. Had you ceased loving me and, frankly and high-minded, had come to me and said that that was the case ... Now, it would have hurt me; but you had neither frankness nor high-mindedness, and now I cannot remember anything other than that you had neither frankness nor high-mindedness. All your joy and pleasure were the evil surprises; and the mirror was your instrument. And now I am outside your range, also spiritually.

◆

Fridtjof turns over onto his other side – where he lies and remembers. The waitress at Morskoi Restaurant – always with clean apron and so pure in countenance – for those attached to the soil in the service of vodka she appeared dimly as a higher revelation. And he thought of his own state of mind in the humbling hours of debasement. The worker who dropped in to Morskoi Restaurant took a glass of vodka and left – a gentleman from a better world he was – for those who are attached to the soil in the service of vodka. And then I had to go home, to a night of sleepless hours, sweat in anxiety so the sheets got wet. ... The mirror, the mirror ...

She always sat there, the woman in the black, greasy dress, the woman who drinks on the sly – pale – for her life was just a bundle of rags, and death a foreign wine, and the castration Christ's literal gospel. She believed Christ walked again with a cross on his back translated to human language: as another half-wit. In this woman's company at the Morskoi Restaurant – and when one too found oneself in the humbling state of debasement, one could in spirit and truth feel as if in the half-light of the nether world. The worker who came, emptied and left, was a gentlemen from a higher world; he went home to Abraham's lap. The waitress with the clean apron was a female angel – none of you can come to us, and none of us to you.

… So Fridtjof had sat in the company of the evangelist at Morskoi Restaurant – stone sober he was; but yesterday it was the mirror and the table setting that had fallen to the floor.

Afterwards he had gone out – around the corner, down a side street, into a courtyard – someone hits him on the elbow at the same moment as he fires.

✦

And now Fridtjof Hooch lies in his fine bed at home with his grandparents and remembers all this; as he has remembered it now every night for eight weeks, he suddenly jumps up and shouts out:

"And this is the irretrievable – I am without sight, without eyes – and am alive!"

And this was the first time this happened to him – that he jumped up, and a cry burst out of him.

Andijn, who had her room next door, came running in.

"Are you ill, Fridtjof?"

"No, not at all! – I was just dreaming; go back to bed!"

***

The morning of the next day attorney Einar Asper came and asked to speak with Mrs. Hooch. He asked her whether there would be a chance to speak with Andijn. Well, she would ask. And she showed him into an empty room. He sat there and waited a good while.

Andijn was pale when she appeared between the drapes. They greeted one another stiffly and politely. Asper to be sure tried to show an agitated cordiality; but it didn't seem to win any sympathy. They sat quiet for a while – on Asper's part it was calculated – which at the same moment he felt a little shamefaced about when the silence didn't seem to make any impression on Andijn.

"I have thought it over back and forth, Andijn – well, what I had to do. If I didn't go to you, then I wouldn't get any peace – and you would misunderstand me – and if I went to you, then you would perhaps interpret it as impudence on my part ... Well, then I had nothing else to do than to try to go to you in the hope of being able to convince you that I meant well. And here I am. Andijn ... I am in any case thankful that you were willing to say hello to me."

"Why would I not want to say hello to you?"

Asper fumbled for words and fingered his watch fob nervously.

"No, you know well that I myself was not in control of it that time. I had been gripped by this anxiety that I was going to get sick – I came under the power of despondency – it was also due to the snowfall and the terrible winter darkness – everything had become so strange to me."

Asper felt that he had begun to be naturally moved; and he was silent, this time sort of with a better conscience.

"But now you are healthy and cheerful again."

"Yes. Yes, that is ..."

And Asper suddenly gets down on his knees in front of Andijn.

"Andijn! There is more I have to confess to you, and which no one else knows. I was not operated on for a tumor on the brain. I've never had a tumor on the brain. I was examined by two specialists; I didn't have a hint of a tumor. But I let people believe that I had been operated on. Oh, don't look so hostilely at me, Andijn. Despise me not for this! ... Andijn, look a little friendly at me if you can. I am healthy. But the winter darkness and snowfall, the strange, desolate land – and – and – and – a woman, a lady, a human being I have known for a long time, and who has in a way played a role in my life – although I have never realized whether I loved ... You will meet her ... Yes. She came together with the winter darkness. Oh, good God – people are thankfully mostly robust. I am not. I really ought never to have traveled up here; but done is done; and I have not been able ... I was and myself became like a helpless witness to everything climbing past my power. If only the distance had not been so great and aimless between us. We humans are pulled and secured only by what is near, become loose from what is distant against our will, no matter how dear it once was. And life is not unoccupied in the interim. Life's reluctance to stick together, it is stronger than us, Andijn."

Asper got up.

"Andijn! ... No, I won't ask you about it."

"About what?"

"I will not ask you whether you believe you could ever forgive me, resign yourself to what has happened."

"No, that is not worth asking about, Einar."

"No, it probably isn't. You are right in that."

"… But that time, Andijn …"

"That time?"

"Yes, that time when I didn't come…"

Einar Asper bursts into sobs like a wounded animal.

"When you were up there and waited for me – and I didn't come."

Andijn gets up.

"You nevertheless couldn't contain yourself from getting into that! Go! Go! Go!"

"I will go – I will go, Andijn, but be patient with me a while. I cannot come tumbling out on the street, with a lump in my throat. I will stay only a short while, Andijn."

Andijn left. Asper stood there catching his breath. Ever and incessantly he had experienced in his thoughts what Andijn must have suffered that time. Sincerely and deeply shaken he had reveled in the thought of it, so all his limbs had become tender – an appalling pleasure in his own and Andijn's indescribable sufferings that time, that time, that time.

Andijn came in again, shaken with cold shudders in the crown of her head.

"But if you ultimately want to know what I experienced that time, then you can gladly hear it. First, I of course believed that you were a wretch, an indescribably low scoundrel who had enough ruthlessness to enjoy such. But then – then – I could do nothing other than to thank destiny that …"

"That you didn't get married to a man who perhaps could become insane at any time."

Andijn burst into tears.

"I wouldn't have said that, Einar!"

Asper, as the glance in his dark eyes sort of seems to swim freely, says:

"Perhaps you got off easier than I had imagined … And then …"

He is silent.

"And then?"

Asper's dark eyes whiten – he says almost threateningly:

"You won't get me to believe that you got off so easily from it as you will give the impression of. Tell me rather everything, everything that you suffered and experienced that time! And then in return I will tell you what I myself suffered and experienced that time, and since. Let us sit down and be candid."

Asper stretches his long arms toward her, grasps her by the shoulders – and then it is suddenly as if something bursts in him – he weeps like a child …

140

"You were right, Andijn, you could thank your God for that. I am a helpless wretch. And now you yourself have in these minutes seen and heard it. Now you will be able to feel yourself free, Andijn. At the most you will be able to have a little compassion for me; now you know that I am not worth so much as a bitter thought. … But they were some terrible days for you, that time, when I didn't come and you had gotten everything ready for the wedding – isn't that so?"

Andijn, who had become afraid, says mildly:

"Yes, that's right, Einar."

"Yes, I can imagine – indeed it had to be frightful. Farewell, Andijn."

And Asper left. Andijn stood in the window. There he walked over the square; the long buttoned cape made his slender, three-ell figure even taller. But God, how his posture and gait were supple and resilient – he walked as if on steel springs.

But suddenly it was clear to Andijn … greedy, droolingly greedy he had with his own ears wanted to hear what she had had to go through that time. For or against his will he had disclosed, that – yes, that it was with these her sufferings torn by grief before the eye he had turned back that time … Poor man!

Andijn stood there as if paralyzed. Then she became cold and disillusioned. She had nothing to accuse him of anymore. And now she wanted to be able to feel free. He maybe didn't know himself what he had said there. Children and people with their minds on life's border do what others recoil from doing: what is terrible and tempts, tempts even God's own.

***

Attorney Toddy-Jakobsen who for years had enjoyed hospitality with Andijn's parents in the inland village right away made a fitting, little party in honor of Andijn – Asper naturally was not there. And here Andijn met that lady who had played so great a role in her life recently, the maiden Signe André, telegrapher, the stranger. Andijn knew ahead of time that she would meet her here. No, it was nothing important now; Andijn knew that Miss André was already as good as engaged to magistrate Ludvig Mæhre. And after the meeting with Asper today Andijn now lived in a fresh and new world of liberation. Before she had been nervous about the unavoidable in standing face to face with Miss Signe André. And Andijn had been consumed with countless plans as to how she should behave and always it had ended with fear that perhaps she nevertheless would not be able to control herself.

They were introduced to each other by Toddy-Jakobsen, and beyond all expectation both succeeded in pretending it was nothing – that is: for Signe André that was obvious, for her, such was innate, she had learned so much in life's depressing school.

Andijn was tall, with a golden sheen in her hair; Signe André was almost tiny and slender, with dark blond hair.

The evening ended with their apparently, though tacitly, having agreed to be friends.

***

But already a couple days later Andijn felt disappointed. Signe André would continue to be a closed book for her.

One day, magistrate Ludvig Mæhre came to the town, and he and Signe André announced their engagement. People were a little surprised at it. And it was that people sort of began to look up to Mæhre, and Mæhre walked around and received congratulations, the tips of his toes pointed upward more than ever. His chronic smile in these days actually became frozen.

But Signe André's attitude toward Asper, the thorn in Mæhre's side, was just as unchanged. She was just as considerate of him, and Mæhre thought he had to put up with it. This too was a closed book for Andijn. Half confused, Andijn also tried to appear courteous towards Asper; but she wasn't able to do it – that is: it wasn't natural for her – but it seemed to be natural for Miss André. No, Andijn could not be included in such: Signe André was closed and indifferent, not Andijn, and Andijn herself conceded that – she felt more and more helpless towards the other. And if she withdrew, Signe André would also be indifferent to that.

***

Otherwise, Andijn took a walk every day with her blind brother. No one who saw them from behind would take Fridtjof Hooch for a blind man; he walked just as lithe and freely as before, only held on quite loosely to his sister's arm. Andijn had to remember what she had dreamt about last winter in good times at home: that she cared for Einar Asper and was good to him, the poor boy. Einar didn't have a tumor on the brain; but with Fridtjof, both eyeballs had been taken out. Now, one could take that as one wanted to; but that's the way it happened one time.

… The town's ladies, both the older and the younger, were busy showing Fridtjof Hooch small courtesies. The young, handsome man who had always been so chivalrous toward women, toward everyone. And who bore a prouder head than he? Never an indecent word. A youth with a spotless reputation.

And then he had gotten involved in all this in Archangel. It was beyond all measure. And then the gloomy, older woman in the black, greasy dress. What was it the skipper had said about someone who called herself a closet drinker; and the ladies whispered to each other about the closet drinkers.

But the ladies though didn't recognize Fridtjof Hooch; and they had become still more shaken. He didn't give a hoot about their attentions, offended them all without consideration. Wanted once and for all to have none of their importunate sympathy and that sort.

"Now I can go for a walk with Fridtjof, so you get a break for a while, Andijn. Take me by the arm, Fridtjof, then we'll walk, it sounded enticingly sweet."

"I'm not a lap dog. And Andijn isn't missing anything."

And the previously so beautiful and proud young man had become downright coarse of mouth, laughed rashly and didn't give the least sign of being despondent. Valiant?

… He said one time to a close friend of his:

"Take it as a hollow affectation or what you will, but I am happier now than before. And it will sound even more hollow to you, when I say that I am happy to avoid seeing mirrors and all of that which before pained me to see. It can be different for other blind people. But with me it is in any case that way. And now I'm almost tempted to laugh when I think of Morskoi Restaurant and the closet-drinking woman in the black, greasy dress. I can still laugh at a certain mirror."

… Halle Bergstrøm, a Swedish Finn, twice bankrupt businessman who had his residence in the middle of town where the hill goes up to the church and right above the bailiff's office and residence, had again come back after having been away a half year in Finland. It was said that he was spying for Russia. A secret sign of that you might also see in that it was hard for him to show enthusiasm for the harbor between the town and the island outside being dredged so that larger ships could come in, and that a proper new stone pier was going to be built. All of that was in itself good enough, and what others wanted. Bergstrøm had undoubtedly his own opinion of this; the harbor and pier should be finished before the enemy one day came.

Bergstrøm had come back early in spring and had a young niece with him from Finland. Lisa was dark eyed and with dark hair; but her face was narrow and nobly formed. Lisa didn't associate with anyone, but was otherwise often with the Kven fishermen out on the sea; she who in a way nevertheless was a woman. She spoke Swedish and Finnish equally well.

All this was also a hidden sign, and Bergstrøm undoubtedly had his own opinion in allowing her to wander from place to place and speak with Kvens.

She was talked about a lot in the town. Fridtjof became interested in his way. He asked his grandmother who had become acquainted with Lisa Bergstrøm to invite her to dinner sometime. But Lisa Bergstrøm didn't seem at all to be so keen on accepting the invitation; she simply didn't come; she was absolutely against playing kind sister to the blind man.

One day Fridtjof is walking up the hill and has come up to the church; Fridtjof hears the steps of a woman coming the opposite way. When the steps had passed by, Fridtjof stops:

"Who is it?"

"It is Miss Lisa Bergstrøm."

Fridtjof turned. Lisa Bergstrøm also happened to look back, and she saw the blind man standing there and looking after her.

The same afternoon Lisa Bergstrøm stood on the steps at the Hooch residence and rang the bell.

And the upshot of it was that Lisa Bergstrøm came to replace Andijn every time Fridtjof was going out on his daily walking tour.

And now Fridtjof Hooch was again the lovable, handsome young man the ladies had known before.

Okto
Alone

Halle Johanas and his friend and Juhas Juhasj and the others are now poling up the river, the tin buckets they have bought at the Midsummer Market shine in the sun. It snarls in the bow of the long, fine Ville Jongo boats; the waves wash away out over the water surface, and in the big poling hours when the men really give an effort, the small waves sing against the gravel banks over on the other side of the river.

They always pole along the shore, and on the same side, these, the best polers on the entire earth, and who have the best riverboats on the entire earth. They stand each on one end of the boat and pole in step, pull in three long steps up the three-fathom long poling sticks, shove just as the whole body is bent backwards – for at the next moment to jerk the pole back, turn it and the body forward, so again the three long steps and a last thrust. It snarls around the bow; and the tin buckets shine in the sun, a smell of flowers comes from the meadows.

So pure are the lines in the boat that they smooth out all the dragging water from themselves.

Juhas Juhasj and Dullerova Jussa pole each in his white shirt with an artistically woven belt around the waist, and they are in white homespun pants. Polers from the inland village ought to and should pole in white shirts and with artistically woven belts around the waist, and the poling sticks must be white. It is by the living God only second-class polers who appear in a dirty shirt or smocks and have poling sticks that are dark gray from age.

All together they dip the upper end of the pole in the water on the outer side of the boat, in order to hold it gliding smooth between the hands.

Dullerova Jussa was born a Kven from the inland village, son of a poor, immigrated couple. He measures his three ells, is straight as a stick, has a sharply cut, narrow face; the glance in his large and somewhat deep-set eyes always

147

takes notice of this or that he looks at with a positively threatening strength, even if it is just a mouse. When Jussa once as a boy complained to his brother that the schoolmaster had given him a spanking, his brother Junti said: "Listen here, Jussa, you should take your teeth and bite the schoolmaster in the seat."

But although Dullerova Jussa was born and raised in the inland village he nevertheless doesn't have the right way of poling, not the way that Juhas Juhasj and Halle Johanas and the others have.

The boat Halle Johanas and his friend have rented is hard to pole – now they should have had Halle Johanas' own! Oh, even Halle Johanas has to swear! They lag behind.

But when they come up to the first little rapids at *Jáguidgieddi*, Jacob's meadow, where the royal road goes over the isthmus to the fjord to the east, they get excited. They pole seemingly at ease. But Juhas and Jussa, who constantly cast a glance back see that the bodies of the two others are like taut sails. Here there is a gravel bottom, a real bottom for the pole sticks. Halle Johanas and his friend are catching up to the boat in front, let out on the outer side, the waves splash in over the gunwale on Juhas and Jussa's boat. The men are silent, and it sings in the bows … But then Dullerova Jussa shouts, who is always afraid for his things:

"The goods are getting wet!"

And the speed is reduced.

✦

That day they had poled the 40 miles from the river mouth up to the Big Chasm.

There are several boat crews that have stopped here for the night. It is still midnight sun, but the reflection of the sun is now only seen up on the mountains. The young bachelors sneaked around the tree house where comely Mar'ja on the riverbank usually slept in the summer. But comely Mar'ja didn't open up.

***

The next morning they pole up the hard stretches below the Big Chasm that roars deafeningly powerful in the narrow, canyon-like run, with sloping rocks and helter-skelter lying heavy stone blocks on both sides.

Lemik Piera who is with Juhas Juhasj and Jussa, sits on a twig bed in the middle of the boat. It is again Jussa's turn to pole. Juhas Juhasj who is sort of a captain always stands down in the stern.

They have gotten right up below the Big Chasm, and up this you always take the Finnish side, since it forms the inside of the turn and it is therefore easier to come up on this side.

For the time being they have gone ashore, in a little backwater behind some stone blocks. But even in here the boat shakes like an aspen leaf; the waves break up heavily and violently in this little backwater.

Dullerova Jussa is pale; but he doesn't want to admit that he more than eagerly saw that Lemik Piera took his turn now. The boat has to be lightened for some of the goods. And now Lemik Piera is nice – he says:

"You, Jussa, you who are young and strong, you can begin to carry the goods upward; I myself would rather pole."

Lemik Piera and Juhas Juhasj choose the strongest pole sticks they have. They drive the boat sideways out into the rapids. At every moment the boat must be held lengthwise with the rapids, with just a slight pointing toward the shore, and Juhasj is always on the watch to hold the stern end a little out. And at the same time they are both on the lookout for a suitable channel between the underwater rocks that thundering masses of water pour over and form a whole ladder of cascades. And out there in the middle of the rapids it thunders earsplittingly; the waves pour around and send up white clouds like breakers during a hurricane.

Lemik Piera doesn't need to look back; he knows that Juhas Juhasj is at his post. Just every so often when they have to go rather far out does he cast an inquisitive look at Juhas, and Juhas nods – a few difficult cascade ledges ahead; they exchange a glance, and in the next moment they send the boat up with a few powerful, long poles. The high and, on top, broad bow lifts the fore end up, and the boat is above the ledges. The waves the whole time have hit inward, and here they have to stop and bail the boat.

Right after come Halle Johanas and his friend; but then Juhas and Lemik Piera hurry to get further, up the rolling, crushing masses of water; they want to be the first to be above the Big Chasm. But Halle Johanas and his friend are gaining on them and they can't resist expressing that they intend to go past. But then Juhas bellows so he even drowns out the roar and noise out there in the rapids:

"*Maid beargalahkii!* – what in the hell! – *rassat guoikkas!* – pole into the rapids!"

***

Above the Big Chasm began the 45 miles that, practically speaking, is a single rapids, just here and there somewhat evenly running currents. A salmon fence here, one there, sometimes on the Finnish and sometimes on the Norwegian side.

The upper and last rapids they passed the next morning. And the 50 miles that were left to the inland village were mostly just an effort in patience to get through – with a couple small exceptions, all even currents. And now a few small pinewoods began to come into view.

But Halle Johanas and his friend's rented boat was too hard to pole – and above the Big Chasm they had to give in and let the others disappear ahead.

And when they leave the national border a few miles below their village and go into the river that is their own, they meet Hooch and his wife who are already on the way down via boat. They had heard from Juhas Juhasj and others what had happened to Fridtjof. Letters? – Yeah, Halle Johanas had them.

And as soon as Hooch recognized Halle Johanas, he broke out into a rage, out of sorts as he was before:

"What sort of idiocy is it that you haven't given the letter to people who can get there! Here you drift like a snail along the river and haven't thought that you had a letter on you that should have been delivered!"

His friend got white with anger and started to bellow out in Sámi; but Halle Johanas asked his friend to be quiet and turned toward Hooch and said:

"I'm not in the habit of making threats, Hooch; but this time I will say: be quick getting away from here, otherwise I will not guarantee what can happen; but remember that we will meet again, and then we will settle up, *Hooká*."

The transport people and Hooch and his wife knew Halle Johanas, and they saw and heard and knew that Halle Johanas stood behind what he had said.

"Yes, row on now for God's sake!" said his wife worried – and they rowed on.

And Halle Johanas and his friend poled on. His friend appeared to be satisfied with what Johanas had said to Hooch. It was of course Andijn's fault that things had gone to hell with their boat in the Big Chasm. But Halle Johanas kept quiet, just poled harder.

From the national border and all the way up to the summer pastures, a few miles above the village, the river went in a regular zigzag between the flat and almost uniform river headlands. The outlying meadows, surrounded by willow brush, were always farthest down on the headlands, since these are lowest and inundated by the spring flood's mud. Farther up are the birch woods, and the pine on the hillsides above. In the inlets below the outer meadows swam one or other mother duck with her numerous offspring, still only with brownish yellow down for covering.

On the lower side of each headland are broad sandbanks, on the upper side steep waves of sand with overhanging trees. The polers always pole over the river at each headland tip – so as to pole below the sandbanks, since the shore water here is deeper; along the sandbanks a wake path will readily form.

Then they catch sight of quite a few boats with their prows pulled a ways up onto the dry area; it is in *Vuotkamohkki*, nine miles below the village, the best salmon spot down here. People are sitting around a couple small bonfires on the grass hill by the gravel bank on the south side this evening of sunshine; the river is shiny and deep here on this curve. A few mosquitos and the aroma of flowers. And a white sandbank sticks out from the headland tip over on the north side. Yes, how delightful it is to sit here and drink coffee, fry salmon on spits, cut slices of dried reindeer meat and let the mouth talk nonsense unconcerned.

Damned if it isn't Juhas Juhasj already salmon fishing down here says Halle Johanas' friend! And how he is expanding on news, he who has been at the Midsummer Market down there. Here there's a lot of talk about the government – about the parliament – *stuorra-digge birra* – og *Sælbulaš*, yeah *Sverdrupa birra* – and about that Fridtjofa who had drunk vodka and wanted to shoot himself to death because a Pomor woman in black clothing had bewitched him and in her closet-drinking Jesus name demanded that Fridtjof should part with his human desire.

But now Erki Lemik Issak and Lukkar Jussa come poling up. The boat is loaded to the gunnels with salmon in half barrels. They have been on a long journey, and they are poling along the shore over on the other side and past. No, you don't stop with such a cargo; you pole on proudly and sort of mysteriously past. People here on the shore become inevitably silent and taciturn. Only Lemik Lemik smiles. He and his old father Læmma Lemik had behaved exactly the same way last week when they came down from the rapids in the west river above the summer pastures, and people at the summer pastures had stood and watched while Lemik Lemik and Læmma Lemik rowed with their boat loaded to the gunnels down over the rapids up there.

But now Juhas Juhasj bursts into laughter:

"Do you remember Anda Piera on the church hill and Nikko last year – when they had loaded their boat with stones and covered it well. And they came proudly and quietly rowing down past the summer pastures – for yet in heaven's name once in their lives to get someone to become suspicious. Never have they on their own caught a single salmon in their lives, never gotten a single suspicious glance from a fellow human! But now they damn well were going to impress people, and to good purpose. Now people were going to cock their heads and say admiringly: *Vuoi* Anda Piera *vuoi!* – *vuoi* Nikko *vuoi* – *oi, oi,* that Anda Piera! And that Nikko! But Lemik and Læmik and Erki Lemik Issak as it happens were going down to the village, they too; they rowed together with Anda Piera and Nikko whom it wasn't possible to get away from. And Lemik Lemik gets an impulse handed on a silver platter by the evil one himself. Greedily and brutally, he starts to look through what Anda Piera and Nikko had in the boat, like another sheriff's deputy. Stones! Just stones! And Lemik Lemik shouts to someone on the riverbank at the village:

'Come and help Anda Piera and Nikko carry up the salmon.'

And during a hell of an uproar they start to carry the stones, roll stones back to Anda Piera on the church hill, get out a couple half barrels and salt down the stones – all while they kind of carefully see to it that curious folks don't get to see all this salmon. It's damn well the most unchristian thing I've seen!"

But now *Bietta áhkká*, Peter's wife goes up, for there were also women fishing for salmon down here:

"Always the sort of people like you, Juhas Juhasj, make fun of us poor people. Look at the sheriff, the old sheriff, he and the other truly well off folks never make fools of poor people! But you and your equals! …"

And *Bietta áhkká* grabbed a grayling that had just been put on a spit over the fire and hit Juhas Juhasj on the mouth with it. And she nearly burst with arrogance when the others began to chortle.

After a half-day's chat they finally start to fasten the various nets together, and then it is Lemik Lemik who says what all the others are thinking about:

"Now the sheriff is at home enjoying himself. We'll put the seine net right across the river." And a couple boats go a ways down and put down some stakes in an oblique row over the river; another boat crew comes with the salmon fence with weights and throws it out while little by little they tie the strong thread at the top of the net to the posts.

And then they all pole a ways upward to sweep the salmon down.

***

The silence in the village now when the haying season hasn't yet begun, it is a beautiful silence. Most are now up at the summer pastures, a few miles above the village, but along the same river. Some have gone salmon fishing up the rapids in the two rivers above the summer pastures, others below.

152

The cottages, washed clean, echo the loom's racket: three rapid bangs with the shaft, and the shuttle flies again running through the warp, and the feet shift over to a couple other treadles below.

The meadows bulge with lush, fine grass; it sways billowing in the wind, and bluebells and daisies sway along.

My God, how these cottages in the village are clean!

The few that are now here always go in their Sunday best, the men in white homespun pants and white jackets with red and blue edges over the shoulders and on the upright-standing collars, the women in jackets of red and blue striped bolster.

Ville Jongo is busy making a new boat in the farmyard. Halle Johanas stands and watches: that boat he would like to have had, but he must also buy a foal for the fall – to buy a horse is out of the question.

***

Olle, Ville Jongo's little son, lies in bed up at the summer pasture – he has again cut himself on the foot while he was hewing some stakes for a little salmon fence in a little side stream that runs out into the big river right below Jongo's summer pasture. He also had a couple scars on his feet from axe blows from before, two or three scars above his knee, from a cut and a stab, a scar on one leg from a cut – not to mention all the scars he had on his right hand – he was left-handed. No, he certainly wasn't clumsy, God only knows, he wasn't. But he was always so immensely busy when he was working on a thing, and could never stop before he had gotten so overworked that he shook. Worked from morning to evening without stop. There was so tremendously much that had to be done.

But in the winter he was often sick, had 'a pain in his chest' and his stomach hurt; he had waded so much in the ice water in spring when the ducks came.

But that was nothing compared to having a headache – as one day here early in summer. Olle had been lying on his back; his older brother came and carried him in. A large reindeer bull was pressing his antlers against his chest – save me!

But that was nothing compared to his seeing the sun disappear right after, huge and with great speed, and Olle has to get down on his hands and is going to catch the sun – is going to catch it – so appallingly frightfully absurd; but he is going to get down on his hands and catch the sun – oh, for heaven's sake, save me from this!

… Then it was over. No, Olle didn't tell anyone what shaking visions he had experienced; it didn't occur to him a single time that he should tell it. What did people know about what a person can suffer.

No, he didn't think about that other vision, the one he had seen many years ago in reality; he was probably no more than six years old that time: a tar barrel was lit at a neighbor's one dark autumn evening. Olle and a couple other small boys are standing and looking at the fire that is burning at the edge of the turf at the bottom. Olle stands turned toward the north; he sees a large fireball travel over the forest ridge on the north side of the river – and with a long glowing tail. The two other boys didn't see it. And Olle was quiet and said nothing. He had never seen anything like that before. But he was quiet and said nothing.

Káfe vuošša II
Coffee Break II

In the middle of October the ice on the rivers and mountain lakes had begun to be passable. There was a large snowfall – then it became mild weather again – and suddenly there was frost again; the slush froze into thick ice and covered moss and heather on the mountain slopes and the mountains.

It was then that the mountain Sámi who had already come back to the inland village became frightened.

"If enough mild weather doesn't come so that the ice cover can melt then it looks bad for those of us from the heights."

But the mild weather waited.

Citizen Sire Andaras' *siida* had come migrating from the north already in September; but they had stayed on the level mountain plateaus on the north side of the valley until the ice on the river had become passable. And now they had again started up the same valley where they had their winter camp last year. Sire Andaras had learned last spring that the moss up there had not been grazed off yet.

But the host people in the first mountain inn on the north side of the valley, some 20 miles from the summer pastures, could hear from the dog baying that there were still *siidas* migrating.

The reindeer went around on the hillsides and tried to find spots that were not covered with ice, and on the hillsides they found a few open spots, and immediately all the animals threw themselves over them. At the next moment even the heather roots had been devoured. It was simply a pity to see the animals bang away on the ice covering with their hooves – without overcoming it – and then it smelled of palate tickling moss beneath! Wild with hunger they went around; it was impossible to keep them together. The dog baying and herder shouts resounded everywhere this fall; but the animals had come under the power of hunger, the herds scattered to the four winds; and many of the calves from last spring toppled over – or had to be slaughtered.

And if there were now to be – *šlubbá* – sickness this winter too, heaven have mercy on us! And *šlubbá* is a sickness in the toe joints of the reindeer.

It was a hard blow that struck the reindeer Sámi this fall – hundreds of reindeer were lost to Sire Andaras and others had suffered similarly large losses too. But for wolves and reindeer thieves along the long valley it was like a big wedding.

Now, no one suffered in these and other inland districts up here; the poor budget was a mere trifle. Housekeeping in nature is so multifarious.

The ice covering forced many reindeer Sámi to move to higher lying plateaus, where the slush had been less dangerous last fall.

***

Only when Sire Andaras' people had set up camp in the valley did her mother ask Elle if she was with child.

… Until now Elle hadn't been able to come to any clear decision about what was to be done. For her own part, she didn't really have so much against marrying Gonge; she had come to be fond of him more and more. But the thought that the tall, malicious Andi Piera with the stallion and other property then would have the opportunity to smack his lips and get revenge on her with derisive words: that she had had to marry Gonge, and that, moreover, under that sort of circumstance. And after her beloved Mikkal had been sent to prison for reindeer theft. Elle, so often sung to, with no less than two yoik melodies, made in praise of her. The thought of all this got Elle to deal with bad, unchristian thoughts.

… Elle and her mother are sitting on an overturned sled outside the tent, her mother says:

"Just say my child how it is."

Elle was as if paralyzed.

"I can't say anything – Yes, I am so …"

… Poor Gonge was conscious of his own lowliness; it hardly occurred to him that he could be married to Elle, let alone how deep and heavy his love for her had become.

… Sire Andaras was completely beside himself when his wife told him what was going on with Elle – and with Gonge!

***

158

It was a difficult journey Sire Andaras made down to the village this time. Elle had become awe-inspiringly furious when her father suggested that Andi Piera would probably be willing to marry her for the ... And as far as Mikkal was concerned: Mikkal had already come back from *Troandin seminara* during the summer. No, Elle didn't seem to care for Mikkal any more now; she seemed almost to be indifferent to the whole thing now.

... Nevertheless, in his distress Sire Andaras one evening in all secrecy visited Andi Piera. Well, let me see ... But Andi Piera had to give vent to his bitterness. Well, now I am good enough for Elle ... now that she's gotten involved in such.

But Sire Andaras didn't want to have anything unfinished. He also visited in all secrecy that Mikkal, so despised by him before. Mikkal was delighted to be able to do Elle that favor, and happy and gratified he said, how she had called to him last winter outside the detention room and said that she loved him and would marry him when he came back. And happy Mikkal harnessed his reindeer to drive up to Sire Andaras' *siida* and talk a little with Elle – for the really big *soagŋu*.

But when Mikkal came, happy and pleased, it dawned on Elle that this was after all what was actually deplorable with Mikkal – yes, Elle was really tempted to laugh: so droll did this sadness of Mikkal seem to her ... No, it wasn't that he had been punished; and she had loved him with a sincere heart last year, also after he had been found guilty. But one thing had little by little become clear to her: Mikkal was a spineless fellow, a rich man's son who stole could somehow not feel well among proper people, handsome and strapping as a prince to look at, but a drunkard and incorrigible coward.

***

And now Andi Piera was confident he was right, now that Mikkal had been dismissed in advance – even before the big *soagŋu*. But it went still worse with Andi Piera on this his courting journey.

***

Andijn had come home now. Fridtjof was still with his grandparents in the town, and his mother was again with him. The idea was that Andijn should be at home just a short while, and travel southward to regain her strength and have diversions in other and larger and new surroundings, something that she too also needed so very much – after all she had experienced the past year.

Andijn took every opportunity she could to meet Halle Johanas. It was solace for her to be together with the fair, slender Halle Johanas, he who had always been so faithful and chivalrous to her, and she could well admit that she was in love with him.

But when Hooch, after having visited Fridtjof in town, came back again in the summer the following happened.

Hooch is sitting in his living room one morning. There is a knock on the door, and in steps Halle Johanas; he has a whip in his hand. Hooch starts up, turns pale. Johanas says:

"I am, as you know, *Hooká*, not a dangerous man. But one thing is inescapable: I must give you a beating."

Hooch moves toward the door, furious, but doesn't want to humiliate himself by calling for help; the maid was for that matter out, and the hired man in the store. Halle Johanas stopped him, and Hooch felt in the grip that resistance was in vain here.

"I don't really know how Norwegians take their pants down; we Sámi have a simple tie in the waistband. You will have to take your pants down yourself – yes, there is nothing else to do, *Hooká*. Yes, make it quick! Or else I'll tear your pants to shreds."

Hooch had suddenly become helpless in mind and body like a small child. He wanted authority.

… And after the punishment Halle Johanas begins to speak.

"I am no hypocrite when I say that I am very sorry that I had to do this. When I ran my horse to death it was the fault of my own dumb weakness. I could not refuse to drive fast and without pause when Andijn asked me to do it. And you had no duty to give me compensation for the horse. But you swore in advance that you would not do it. Oh, there was something else, *Hooká*. When I came back this summer with my rented boat, Juhas Juhasj told me that you had found out that my boat had been smashed in the Big Chasm, because Andijn, at the very last second, wanted to go ashore, and I couldn't, was not able to refuse rowing her ashore. I would not have told you this myself; I myself would have kept the whole thing concealed. But you found out from others, and then you swore too that it was my own business when I was so dumb. And it was after you had found out about this that you came out with offensive, abusive language to me when I met you on the river down there. You were of course justified then; you had received an agonizingly sad message, and you had experienced a lot on Andijn's behalf last winter. And besides we all know here in town that you are an honorable man, an embellishment for our village; and we have all been fond of you. But it has turned out that I have had to suffer insults on your part, without you perhaps knowing it yourself or made a point of hurting me. I suffered patiently with this for a long time; but I began to understand that I would end up being a poor human being in my heart and mind and in others' eyes if I didn't make a discernible revolt. Now I have done it; you have gotten a good beating, and now you are crying. But it is still perceived by me in such a way that it is not cleansing enough for me that only you and I know what has happened here in your own house. I must also tell it to others, and I must advise you not to deny it; for otherwise I will have to do the same thing again in the presence of others."

✦

This happened last summer.

But Andijn used every occasion she could to talk to Halle Johanas.

And besides she had experienced a great relief recently: the last mail had brought the news that Signe André and magistrate Ludvig Mæhre had gotten married, an event that, for that matter, otherwise didn't inspire much interest among the upper classes down there. Ludvig Mæhre had never interested anyone, and now Signe André too had disappeared into his uninteresting atmosphere … Consciously, Andijn's heart was dead towards Einar Asper; but she discovered nevertheless that the news relieved her. – Signe André had, all the same, right to the very last been a gallstone in her heart.

***

Ågall and his daughter Anga also came up to the inland village this Christmas. And now people were witness to something they had never imagined: Jørgensen the sheriff's deputy had become best friends with Anga – and even with Ågall himself too! For if Ågall last winter hadn't bewitched Jørgensen the sheriff's deputy, then this poor sinner himself would have had to lock himself into the detention room in the middle of the night and sit there until it began to get light outside. And before people realized, it was a fact that Ågall's daughter and Jørgensen the sheriff's deputy were going to get married! Now people were not certain whether Anga would be considered Norwegian or Sámi: both Ågall himself and Anga wore Sámi costumes daily, and her mother was no doubt Sámi or maybe Kven. Ågall himself, the sorcerer with the owl face, was certainly Norwegian. As beautiful and fair and tall as Anga was it was nevertheless that ordinary bachelors among the people didn't dare to want her. But Jørgensen the sheriff's deputy did, and he wagged his tail like a beaten dog for Ågall – Ågall who had conjured him into detention a couple of nights last year. And people spoke so somberly about this, viewed also from that side that Anga was going to marry such a despised person as Jørgensen the sheriff's deputy – maybe a little punishment from the Lord for her father's having practiced sorcery throughout a long life. Although it was also said that Ågall was a Christian and didn't practice his deeds out of evil, but so that justice should happen adequately.

Jørgensen the sheriff's deputy had otherwise already last summer started building his own house; he wanted to start a little business here too – run it alongside what little he had in one of the fishing stations far to the northeast.

Every evening this summer and fall he had gotten boys and others who were out and about where people were working, to lend him a hand for fun, carry rocks to the foundation wall, saw, trim wood; and the boys thought that was fun – there were always so many gathered and had a chat – and Jørgensen the sheriff's deputy was charming in every way. And it was unbelievably much he had gotten the young boys to achieve for fun in the course of the fall.

… Also Elle felt it a relief that Anga in any case was not going to marry Mikkal – that Mikkal she herself didn't want to have – in spite of his situation. Yes, for Anga with her closed face had caused her so many silent sufferings last year when Elle still was in love with Mikkal.

***

At the end of February Elle had a baby boy – he was born in the attic of Erki Lemmik Issak, and where Sire Andaras' people usually lived when they were down here in the village during the winter. The birth was extremely easy; there was almost nothing other than a few sighs to be heard from her.

… A few weeks later – "may the heavens consume the pancakes!" said Juhas Juhasj! Then Andi Piera came on *soagŋu*, with a large escort, to Elle! Really again! Have you ever seen such a persistent and determined person.

Elle sat on the edge of the bed with the baby in her lap. The attic room was chock full of spectators, also the steps and the room below.

And now people got to see for themselves that Andi Piera had property. His spokesman, Jouna Jouna, John Johnsen, made a grand courting speech: Elle, whose draft reindeer was sailing like a ship at full sail, the only child of rich Sire Andaras, pretty as a gosling that still has only its yellow, fine down, courted like no other – and then *dállubárdni*, the farm son Andi Piera, what bachelor has property as he does, the largest stallion in the village, a cow barn and stable, and house almost finished, a proud name Andi Piera has! Yes, there will be couples to stand in awe of. Reindeer herd and farm, can carry mail in the winter, sail with timber rafts in spring and fish salmon in summer, who else has such a riverboat as Andi Piera?

And Jouna Jouna poured into a silver beaker. Sire Andaras drank from it, his wife Zare drank from it – but Elle – not at all! Not at all! Andi Piera's mother loosened the bundle of gifts, jingling gold rings and silver brooches, silk and woolen shawls – and forced them into Elle's lap. But the baby filled Elle's lap; she held tight to the baby on her lap, and pushed the gifts away with one hand. The *soagŋu* people and spectators were getting agitated: some of them sided with Elle, others with Andi Piera – there has to be a limit to being arrogant too! – When one in addition sits with a baby in her lap.

It ended with Andi Piera's mother losing her patience:

"The hell with Elle and her baby! My son can get whomever he wants – rich Bækka on the other side of the neighborhood has a daughter too, and she doesn't have a child! – And Bækka is the richest mountain Sámi in both kingdoms."

And the courting people headed out.

***

But a couple weeks before it again became Easter people got to view an eyesight. Gonge, the hired hand with Sire Andaras, and who otherwise was a pure forest troll to look at, when he very seldom showed up in the village. An unkempt looking giant with long hair. Gonge, Gonge was a vision! Decked out from head to toe, washed sparkling clean, hair and beard trimmed – in snow white Sámi reindeer boots, in leggings of shining black, short-haired leather from the forelegs of the reindeer and around the ankles the leggings were lengthened with a broad scarlet cloth, wound around with an artistically woven band, reindeer coat of the finest black reindeer calfskin and scarlet cloth along the upright collar lengthened with two long loops down over the chest. The otter-skin cap with the star-shaped crown filled with down was brand new and at the bottom edged with white ermine. And a golden belt around the waist!

He caused pure dismay! And worthy as a sexton! But his deep voice sounded as if he was going to speak in a closed well. Finally, Juhas Juhasj had to laugh – and then everyone laughed.

But they didn't laugh any more when Gongo held *soagŋu* – it had to be done – and the courting people went to the minister, and the Sunday following it was announced for the first time.

Now everyone understood why Elle had been in love with Gonge, and Elle was now more then ever in love with him. Even Sire Andaras had been mildly disposed.

Now there was no end to people's enthusiasm for Gonge; they cocked their heads and said admiring: *vuoi* Gonge *vuoi*:

… During the wedding Elle wore a bridal crown formed right on her head of gold and silver colored metal inlaid band, and silk shawls over her shoulders, brooches on her chest, and a multitude of rings on her fingers. The whole bridal procession was in black homespun jackets, and the bridegroom and the two train bearers had white bands that went around the jacket collars, in a cross over the chest and with the ends stuck beneath the gold belt around the waist. The two bridesmaids wore a helmet-like head covering, and on the helmet's back-side were tied long bows of various colored silk bands.

… Erki Lemik Isak's large barn kettle was filled again and again with meat, and steaming wooden bowls were carried into the house. After the wedding Elle and Gonge went around the village each with a bottle and silver goblet and invited guests.

Later in the afternoon the first yoik melodies were heard; the many emptied silver goblets had had their effect. The yoiking became louder and louder. A boy and a girl from the wild West Plateau district stood and yoiked in antiphony, the boy held on to the flaps of the girl's silk kerchief, and she to his lasso; it was just like a boy from the West Plateau district to wear a lasso and the large sheath knife at a wedding! They yoiked and yoiked, swayed with their bodies back and forth in step; at times they both yoiked together, then again alternately – their faces flushed more and more, they looked each other in the eyes, and finally they yoiked with a wild joy and enraptured delight as if they had been two alone in the wilderness one spring evening and had given each other all life's joy and ecstasy.

… Later in the evening the table in the large room was cleared and covered with a big red shawl; the bridal couple sat down at the upper end and the master of ceremonies, Lemik Lemik, took his place standing at the side, with a bottle in one hand and a silver goblet in the other.

"Well, well, welcome to everyone who wants to give the bridal couple proof of their friendship."

164

Sire Andaras stepped forth first. He pulled a large and thick wallet of leather up from his jacket breast – laid 500 kroner on the table, on behalf of his wife and himself. The guests who were standing tightly packed into the big room, stretched their necks – and high-pitched cries could be heard – *gea!* – see! – five hundred kroner!

Lemik Lemik handed him the goblet and held an impressive speech for Sire Andaras; it was an absolute bank that had been laid on the table! But now Sire Andaras whispered something in his spokesman's ear. Lemik Lemik exclaims:

No, now I almost don't know what I shall say! Sire Andaras says he is giving Elle two hundred reindeer! Before we have called you half jokingly citizen Sire Andaras; hereafter, we'll call you that in honesty. Elle, it is your father who is standing here. And you, Gonge, you have made that happiness in life that you anyway have earned, but which has not been granted many in this world.

And the gifts continued to stream in; the table started to bend from the bills and shiny two-kroner coins. Lemik Lemik poured and poured and his eloquence flourished in all its glory. A small pale and dark eyed boy popped up and laid one krone on the table. Lemik Lemik poured him a quarter goblet and whispered to him: *ollu giitu!* – Many thanks! Olle fell back, very troubled that Lemik Lemik had not held a thank you speech for him. But Olle who had again been sick and bedridden had not drunk his quarter-cup without consequence: it felt so warm and runny in his body – oh, how one could become healthy and bold from a nip! He cleared a path up to Elle and whispered to her:

"I'm going to make a little sled for your baby."

Oh, how Elle's thank-you and smile made him happy. He was of course an old admirer of her. She asked Lemik Lemik to pour a goblet. Olle got one half nip … Olle reeled outside tipsy and bragged and gave speeches. His father came and carried him home – by then he was more dead than alive.

But it caused great astonishment among the guests to see Sire Andaras, citizen Sire Andaras himself intoxicated. In itself it could surely have been excusable; it was after all his only child's wedding. But his handsome narrow face had become more and more distorted; his pure blue eyes had taken on a malicious expression. And he said – so that several of the guests heard it:

"Now I'm going to Andi Piera and ask him to take me for a ride through the village on his the big black stallion. For I don't want to sit here and be Gonge's, my hired hand's guest."

His wife hushed him; but he said:

"Go away, old woman!"

He had never before said that sort of thing to his wife. But Elle and Gonge fortunately didn't hear what Sire Andaras sat talking about. But they would probably get to hear it sometime – what he had said during the wedding party.

… Olle lay sick the morning after. His father came over to his bed, looked at him saddened and said: poor boy. And his father went away again.

***

No, Andijn had not happened to travel southward again, although her father had steadily persuaded her to go. She had taken a trip down to the town to the east this winter – to see Fridtjof – but she had come back again. And now and then, when she was on her daily stroll up the village she went inside Halle Johanas' home.

Skilžiráhkesvuohta
Love for Icicles

It is a couple years later. Miss Signe Mæhre stands in front of the mirror in the magistrate's residence by the river mouth. She is in her prettiest summer dress, is going out to look at the Midsummer Market and then walk past the courtroom. There was court here now during the day, and Einar Aspar was the defense attorney in a criminal case: just think that Einar can still really be appointed to such! Miss Signe hasn't seen him since she got married, has avoided meeting him – nor has she been in the town by the fjord since. She had felt enough whispering in the time she was there …

If she meets Einar now – well – she could not possibly act as if nothing has happened, and say hello to him as a good, old friend. Although – would that be correct? That would disappoint him, seeing that he surely expects that the meeting will make an impression on her. Einar would be moved when he saw that she got a tinge of blood in her face.

She looked in the mirror. She was almost just as slender and supple as two years ago, although she had a child now – a little girl – and who thank heavens didn't look like Ludvig. But something of the earlier pure, soft radiance in Miss Signe's large, blue eyes was sort of gone now.

Now, however it had been with her and Ludvig, she in any case defended him from the external world. Worse it would have been to defend him from her own and fortunately often-quiescent ill will toward him. On those days that for her were gloomily pious – when Einar was in her thoughts – then she closed her heart to Mr. Ludvig Mæhre, refused his caresses, couldn't even stand his hand touching her. But on those days her father lived in her consciousness, the drunken and down-and-out former lawyer in Oslo. It had happened that her schoolmates in her own presence had dropped hints to her father – and she had felt defenseless, cruelly hurt and lost. Others had been busy being democratically kind to her: "It's too bad for her that she has that poor man for her father." And similar difficulties she had had to struggle with too when she became an adult, and which were not more gracious when the men felt and experienced that she was a woman, and the principled woman who only with her silent, proud bearing could get them to be silenced.

But how Einar had been splendid too in this respect! In his own open way he had said, without in the least way trying to be gentle and immediately careful. Damn it all, Signe, he had said once: what would you prefer: either to have an irreproachable, average man with a simple aspect for a father, or a handsome, talented man, whom the joy of life had accidently run away with? Assuming that you in the first case had had to be carried along with the irreproachable, average man's simple aspect and average brain and humble mind, but that you in the second case were blessed with the handsome, talented, but in the gone-to-the-dogs father's proud, god-born countenance – such as is the actual case also for you. Your father at one time didn't have that tough character that saves most men from being pulled along by the joie de vivre cyclones that prevail in the world of the analeptics. But he has produced you. A single human being, created in God's successful image, is worth many times more in God's own display than the hundred others that God has deliberately neglected to make into masterpieces, for the reason that he has great need of unfinished material. Of course, fortunate are those people who in one and the same person have beauty, talent and character. But fortunately there are so few of them, and we avoid falling asleep in a paradise where everyone gapes in an idiotically empty happiness over his own beauty, talent and character. If lions and Bengal tigers and golden eagles were more fertile themselves, then God damn you for your views on the irregular verbs – which it says someplace in Carlyle. How should the people in the warm districts shore themselves up, if they didn't have snakes and crocodiles, scorpions and tigers and deserts and the whole nuisance to hold ones interest – they would die otherwise with their stomachs in the air – what we all do in the end. The devil and hell is not anything humans have discovered in their stupidity and brutality, no, they were so damned necessary to be discovered, and have been equally useful as the steamship in our time.

***

Miss Signy took a long stroll, was almost all the way down to Jarholmen. On the way back she walked past the schoolhouse where the court is held. She felt good that both Einar and Ludvig saw her, and that they were both certain why she walked by here. She came home and sat down without taking her hat off. The maid was with the little tot down at the harbor.

… Claptrap! Just claptrap! Everything Einar had said about her and her father that time. Nothing is so empty as beautiful words of consolation. Life itself doesn't know about excuses. But perhaps it was only a crafty way of touching upon her life, Einar had chosen this method; for Einar liked to revel in the direct vision of such, to read it right out of the face, shout the helpless words into ones ears. Einar could be that way.

… So hopelessly impossible it had been for her to learn whether he loved her or not, although down there she had belonged to him an entire year. Oh sure, he had loved her all right; Einar couldn't feign that sort of thing. But right from the beginning she had noticed that deep inside he was an unhappy man; he had such a penchant for arranging the depressing for himself and others, not anything directly brutal like that, but sort of slowly and at a distance.

Ludvig didn't come home until three.

They sat at the dining room table.

"I saw you walk by the schoolhouse this morning, he said, with a somewhat muddy voice."

"Yes, I did. Now, how is it going with Einar?" Whether she said Einar intentionally or out of fright, she didn't really know herself; but she didn't regret that she had said Einar.

"Just fine – I assume; I didn't have time to speak with him privately."

"You could have invited him home for dinner."

Ludvig sat and stared intently and stiffly at the piece of salmon he had on his plate. At this moment he considered whether he should bang on the table or put on a good face. He chose the latter, which he, as said, always had done in Oslo too when it concerned Einar.

"I couldn't know that you were prepared to have a stranger for dinner."

"Einar is certainly no stranger."

The maid came in with a letter. Invitation to an improvised evening party at Elnagården with the Rudolph Greiners.

"I have four cases to prepare; impossible for me to go to a party this evening."

"As you will."

The rest of the meal was eaten in silence.

… Miss Signe had begun to change her clothes; but now she felt so agitated that she would have sent a rejection if it hadn't been that she didn't want to humiliate herself in front of Ludvig ... Oh, he knew well what he was doing when he decided to stay home and let her go alone. Ludvig had his strength in that sort of thing – when he could make the immediate gestures, then he was at his peak. He knew that she, by going alone, would be humiliated opposite Einar.

The grief got the upper hand. She looked in the mirror: her dress sat crooked, her face agitated. Miss Signe broke into tears. Oh, Ludvig was devoid of the ability to be part of what was interesting; his only force was the small, spiteful evasions. He was always sort of on the watch, always attacked someone sort of in ambush, without warning. The unhappy fifth wheel he had always been in Christiania; up here and as magistrate he should still have been able to assert himself; but there wasn't a soul who paid heed to him here either. He tried enough, but his staring aspect with the long eyes and his cunning unpredictability always made him so unsympathetic. Oh, how she had suffered under this; and yet she had to try to protect him.

Ludvig came in.

"I think I can go all the same – the rest of the work I can do tomorrow morning early."

"But now I can't go!" And Miss Signe broke into tears again, "Because you have destroyed the whole day for me with your cunning ideas."

"And I who thought I was going to make you happy by saying that I could go all the same."

"Go alone, you! And say hello to Einar! And besides I'm going south with the next steamship."

Miss Signe had to go to bed, sick, really sick as she had become.

... She struggles with the nightmare completely awake, suffers purely physically too, knows so fervently well that only by sitting face to face with Einar would she now be able to be freed from this purgatory. But she has stared at herself in the mirror – she looks so frightful – no, rather she struggles with all indescribable agonies than that Einar should see her this way. It was another matter whether she now lay on her deathbed.

... Then she awakens in the morning of the third court day. No, Einar hadn't left yet. And she perceives the bright comfort of convalescence in her mind and body. No, when all is said and done, she couldn't say that it had been an unhappy marriage ... good God, Ludvig could be awkward and seem unsympathetic to strangers; but there were two in him. And how he had striven to try to be good to her! And win her love. And he had certainly suffered more than she suspected – would suspect.

So overpowering had this morning light mood affected her that she broke into tears from pure gratitude toward life, tender and susceptible as she had become in these days.

But she had to travel south; that couldn't be changed. Now, while she was still lucid … she wanted to talk to Einar today; she had a certain presentiment that he too was going to travel while he was still lucid. Oh, now she wanted advice about being genuinely good to Ludvig, – so they could separate without bitterness, yield in humility to this – to this that where life doesn't hang together, there our embraces and our calls for help are of no use – you drift away from each other.

And Ludvig Mæhre had a happy morning, for Signe had not yet dared to tell him what lay behind this her bright conciliatory spirit: that she was going to travel.

"Shall we ask Einar to breakfast!" Ludvig says.

Miss Signe is taken aback.

"… No, I don't think we should do that," she says. "And besides I need a little morning stroll."

And she put on clothes and went out; it is freezing cold and overcast today. Outside Elnagården she meets Einar.

… They followed the smooth road that led up to a little district of a few small farms on the broad and long and entirely smooth slope with birch woods farther up, and then led to the foot of a leaning and steep mountain with rock-strewn slope on the west side.

Einar had come in spirit, had been moved – and when they stopped, he stood there like a broken-hearted person.

"You had heard that I had been engaged to a woman from the inland, Miss Andijn Hooch, and yet you traveled up here, and just when it became the worst winter darkness. I still remember that it was the third of November; you came almost three years ago … Do you remember, Signe, that Sunday I took leave of you – and traveled up the valley, to get married to my fiancée?"

"But, good grief, Einar! Why talk about the snow that fell last year?"

"No, but – no, I can't get rid of this nightmare, Signe. I have to talk about it with you, to try to get rid of it. You refused that time, but I know that it was for my sake you had traveled up here."

"Are you so sure of that, Einar?"

"You are saying this to hurt me – to destroy me!"

"I haven't said anything. I asked you only whether you were sure that it was for your sake I came."

He looked at her terrified.

"Yes, was it then for Ludvig's sake, you came? … Say it, say it, say it immediately, Signe!"

But Miss Signe kept quiet.

"And it had no effect on you when I traveled up the valley to – to get married to Andijn?"

"Yes, it had an effect on me – it made me angry."

Einar wanted to embrace her when he said:

"And you hurt terribly? Didn't you?"

"Not as much as you think," and she pushed him away from herself:

"Not as much as I think? Are you being honest, Signe?"

Miss Signe kept quiet.

"Signe! … Signe! … I feel so good now, that is, I feel so strong and fresh now. Let us – while there is still time – let us run away together. Let us travel south, you and I – Einar reached for her hands. – Let us do it, Signe!"

Miss Signe stood and looked him in the eyes; her look was both aghast and strong.

"No! No, Einar! I will never go with you!"

And she sort of had to listen to her own words and she felt that now it was done … now it was said.

Einar Asper collapsed, his long figure stooped.

"Yes, so you therefore don't love me any more."

"You think surely that the world has stood still for me while it has moved for you."

Einar Asper walks a few fumbling steps around – and looks at the ground beneath him – it looked like he wanted to lie down. Then he says:

"Let's go home, Signe … I feel so tired."

They had walked a few hundred steps – then Einar collapsed … A Sámi came walking down with a cart; Signe and the Sámi lifted Einar up into the cart.

Einar was carried into his room in Elnagården.

Signe sits in a chair by his bed. Einar lies unconscious. But he fantasizes now and then. He rides up the ice on the river; it is dark, but there is still some light … Oh, Lord Jesus, how terrible it would be for Andijn if I turned back … Day after day she would stand still on the steps and listen for whether she might hear the sound of the sleigh bells … There is a little sound; but it isn't my sleigh bells. Then the night comes – and I haven't come yet … there is the letter, my letter. No, I didn't have the heart to let you know the truth right away … Try to tell me, Andijn, how terribly bad it was for you that time. Give me a glimpse of the bottom of the abyss itself! … Something red is running through me, steadily, steadily.

… Signe sat by his bed the next day too. Then Einar Asper opens his eyes. His withered hand fumbles for hers.

"God bless you, little Signe! You were good to me until the end."

And Einar Asper passed away – forever.

***

Inundations of water come from near and far regions – one day it started growing on the sandy soil. And you can build your house on it.

… One time it happened to Signe that she got tears in her eyes when she saw the calm light that now and then could glide over Ludvig's face. But then she sort of kept a watch on herself; it wasn't natural for her to give in to an agitation.

Life can heal where one least expects that it could heal.

Gánda
Boy

Lisa Bergstrøm and Fridtjof Hooch had been married for a couple years now too.

When Lisa was pregnant last year, people in the town to the east hadn't seen an odder marvel: Lisa was in the seventh or eighth month, and only now had her fresh beauty come into its own; she had become an entirely understandable revelation of herself.

And now Lisa had difficulty shielding the child from kissing and fondling by the women. Everyone wanted to look down in the baby carriage or baby sled when she was out with the little one, who was a girl. Fridtjof Hooch's manly handsome countenance had been transformed into a little, charming female image in a cradle.

Even a blind man can get so much good fortune that his blindness no longer seems to be an apology. It could happen that one or another woman rather directly asked Lisa how she actually got along with the blind man; it could surely often be rather difficult? Well, good grief, one had to take it as it was — when one had first tied oneself to a blind man's fate. And a Christian deed it was too. God would reward Lisa to be sure for her willingness to sacrifice herself for him. Lisa gave them the only answer there was to give: She looked at the kind angel in question with quiet contempt.

It had originally been the idea; and therefore Fridtjof too had taken an apprentice position in Archangel to learn Russian that he was going to go into grandfather's business and then take it over, when the old one had died. But — yes, Fridtjof said it himself this way: I learned too much Russian in Archangel to be able to take over any business.

He was a carpenter during the winter — as a boy he had had fun doing joiner's work at Ville Jongo's workshop at home. And during the spring he worked at grandfather's fish business by the fjord further out on the north side: cleaned and salted fish on the dock and in the storehouse, hung up whole fish on the drying racks and could also go along at sea as a rower.

But otherwise he too had become another person for his environment. The previously so serious and sensitive youth had become a robust and, in his mouth, a very careless man. And there were those, in any case among the women, who thought that Fridtjof ought to remember that if God had spared him once or twice and showed him his grace in life, then he ought not forget to be thankful, for he seemed to have become ungrateful, both toward God and his fellow humans who had all wished him well.

Here early last spring before he went to the fishing business outside, he had simply gone into the liquor store, frequented besides by some of the town's better citizens, since the liquor store lay so dominantly central and was the town's only place of entertainment. And Fridtjof had sat there together with Kvens and Sámi and others. Like other business people here in these parts he spoke Kven and Sámi and Russian fluently. He had even at one time in his youth spoken Sámi almost better than Norwegian. Whether it was due to an uncontrollable need to tear himself loose and arouse indignation or whether it was the memory of the Morskoi restaurant in Archangel and the woman in the black, greasy dress, the closet drinkers' priestess – yes, if it was that that rendered him impotent, enough of that: Fridtjof drank himself drunk, told popular, crude stories and treated and treated everyone to drinks. He ended up with a couple of Kvens out on one of the docks, where Fridjof started to struggle with one of the Kvens and went over the edge of the dock, swam around and managed to crawl up again by himself.

But now it depended on whether he noticed that it could have been a warning, it was said.

… In the districts around the national border over on the south side of the fjord, inside the mouth of the fjord way out, there are large and rich pine forests, a magnificent plant life that only inland districts in the more southerly latitudes can compare to and a teeming bird life in the spring – around that river that comes from the south, from Finland. People thought too there were layers of iron in these parts.

A ways above the river mouth here resided a giant of a sheriff, an autocrat by birth, a storm when something was wrong. His farm was somewhat of a manor, and his family had earlier owned a veritable estate farthest in by a long fjord in the country's western part – also by a river mouth, with forests around.

Knach was the giant's name, and the Knach family had through earlier marriages become related to the Hooch family in the two towns on the north side of this fjord here to the east and with the Heemskark family at the bottom of the fjord. Knach's nose could match that of the Heemskarks in height, and Knach had beautiful daughters. And beautiful women open their closed, distant regions to the world and gather destinies around themselves.

To the neighboring kingdom belonged a little piece of land on the otherwise Norwegian side of the river, and here was a Greek-Russian chapel, the pure display of God's gold and silver and other marvelous metals in all colors and shapes – and of silk and brocade. The minister at the chapel was an old red-bearded wine leech, and the congregation a small, shrunken and as good as lifeless remnant of splintered Sámi whose language the other Sámi didn't understand, and who in silence lived in their small timber houses and didn't seem to have anything else in prospect under this God's heaven than that they one by one were going to be covered by the earth's soil. But the sanctuary itself was a little old cabin near the chapel with God's gold and silver – and had been a refuge for two men of God of highborn family in the first Christian assembly up here. The new era's powerful lords who determined the border here took off their hat to the little cabin of a sanctuary and the little, lifeless congregation. They didn't want to sweep it and them over the river, but let them stay on the piece of land they were on.

Fridtjof and Lisa had built for themselves a little summer cabin here along this river, a good ways above Knach's manor. And here Fridtjof had hit on stuffing birds and sending them south to sell. An old hunter, a Sámi, shot specimens for him – and also brought him good wooden raw material from the forest. Fridtjof did a little carpentry here too.

Lisa was soon going to have a baby again. Lisa, who was Finnish you know, enjoyed herself among the many Kvens in this border village and was always ready to help people with supplies and deeds. One afternoon late in August she had rowed over the river to buy salmon and dried reindeer meat. In her current condition she had gotten such an uncontrollable desire for dried reindeer meat. Over there she had run into someone who was sick, and she was delayed there until far into the evening. It was pitch-dark already when she went down to the shore. But Lisa was used to traveling alone. She shoved the boat out and began to row homeward. In the middle of the river she became aware of an odd gleam of light in the air. She turns around: flames of fire are pouring out of the window of their cabin. Lisa gets down on her knees – oh, merciful God, give us your help! Lord Jesus, don't let this happen!

And Lisa takes hold of the oars again – rows, rows – pregnant, but rows upliftingly light and feels nothing of the exertion – merciful God! Save Fridtjof and little Lisa! … The gleam of fire bursts out hectic, and she again has to turn around … only in the next moment to row again, but so upliftingly light does she row, it is as if the boat gets nowhere, and now in the darkness. Only when it bumps into land did she understand that she was there. She ran ashore and up the hill … There outside, Fridtjof is walking with little Lisa in his arms and fumbling away from the burning cabin as best he can. Lisa shouted and ran right up, embraced them both and sank to the ground in a faint.

People from the neighborhood below came running; but they had nothing else to do than to watch the cabin burning down.

… Fridtjof had been lighting the lamp on the carpenter's bench to set it in the window so Lisa could have this light to row toward. And then in one way or other the shavings had caught fire.

***

The following year they built a new cabin on the same site. Fridtjof had perhaps also had the feeling here that he was probably a little bold when he said that it was on the ruins they should preferably build. Now, however that may be, he did it.

Lisa had gotten her second child one and a half months after this fire. To begin with the women in the town were again full of delight: oh, what a lovely baby! Little Hendrik named after Fridtjof's father in the inland village.

But the fire had been a new warning to Fridtjof that could not be mistaken. And it was probably a delusion of his to think that because he was blind he didn't therefore have the right to fence himself in with arrogance and be engaged in frivolous ridicule and sport, as he always had done since he became blind. And he ought not forget how he had become blind. And that was probably all too true, all that had been told about his life in Archangel. Such as his association with the gloomy, closet-drinking woman who was always sitting in the equally gloomy and always half empty Morskoi Restaurant. And if the indignation really flared up, people also spoke about the two little ones. God forbid that they had not become so angelic only that life would be the more dangerous for them; for it could happen that if Fridtjof perhaps himself, in any case apparently was spared the full consequences of the way he had become blind, then – no, may God just not let it affect the two innocent little ones, when they one time would grapple with the difficult life that their beauty perhaps would come to cause them.

One or other sympathetic woman could one day say the remark to Fridtjof Hooch that it was too bad that he could not see these two beautiful children of his. It might be perhaps forgivable that Fridtjof once deigned to give a woman whose children had an insignificant external appearance an insignificant answer:

"Yes, just as bad as it is that you can see your own children, madam."

But that evening Fridtjof also sat at home and cried – for the first time since that accident struck him. How low down can we humans get! Is it so singular that life's Lord ever and always must let his disfavor go out over us, overturn a fear of just and unjust. More than the great misdeeds is the snail spit we part with that leads us to where there are tears and the gnashing of teeth.

Otherwise, there was an evening when he was sitting together with an old, good friend. The friend made a cautious remark that he had never seen his wife.

"No, seen her, such I never have – and it is obvious in its way a loss for me. But you have no idea how I see her anyways! The feeling in me has of course become more strongly developed at this time: through my hands I have a living picture of her face and person. But the best thing is that I see the expression in her face, in her eyes – I feel it when she smiles, even when she says nothing; see when now and then she is tired and sad; see her gait and posture. Yes, God knows, whether I don't have a more living picture of her in my mind now than if I had been able to see her."

… But otherwise Fridtjof Hooch was the same cheerful and careless and arrogant man he had become and had been since that evening when he left the woman in the greasy, black dress in Morskoi restaurant in Archangel.

The minister who had gotten tired of hearing all this talk about Fridtjof Hooch's frivolous arrogance once said that bloody not did God have anything against a blind man being arrogant per se!

Duoddarii
To the Mountains

Like the imposing hard worker that Jørgensen the sheriff's deputy was, he had in the course of a couple years gotten built a solid house and a nice little business in the inland village, and had continued being a sort of private sheriff's deputy for his uncle. From early in the morning to late at night he was on the move, dug in the ground, built, did carpentry, peddled goods, and in spite of being despised he nevertheless was able to get one or other person to work so to speak for free for him.

No one becomes a prophet in his fatherland; and the sorcerer Ågall seemed to have completely lost his power over his son-in-law Jørgengen. Jørgensen did not let himself be duped by the old rascal; it was just damned rubbish that Ågall that time had gotten him to lock himself into the detention room. And his wife, Anga, was steadily reminded that she was only the daughter of the old charlatan who dealt in evil spirits and similar humbug. After two years' marriage Anga had become a quivering aspen leaf. And even though she was pregnant now she had such a fear of taking a little rest. She wore Norwegian clothes now; Jørgensen, before they got married, had demanded that she be wholly Norwegian – which was not at all difficult for her; her father was in all likelihood entirely Norwegian by birth; her mother was to be sure Sámi, but of those who really aren't that so much by blood. And Anga was a real lady to look at: beautiful, tall and stately and naturally dignified – she only had this fateful lack of schooling. And Jørgensen who had always dreamt of being married to a lady with middle school exam! Or at least once in his life to have a lady with middle school exam – even if just for a night. Which though was never to befall Jørgensen.

But no one could deny his sense of beauty: his farmhouse was inside and outside a true example of a beautiful and worthy home. And he was absolutely grand when it counts; he spared nothing to give his home a cultured stamp, and they were not gewgaws and other gaudy finery he had raked together. Jørgensen really had what one calls cultural instinct in this respect. And not before the special wine cellar was ready did he consecrate it by placing at the wall five bottles of champagne, a few bottles of really good cognac, some bottles of port wine, madeira, burgundy and such – as the nucleus; he intended to increase it little by little. But then he also locked the door to the cellar and put the key ring in his pocket; and no one other than he himself could come down into the cellar – he would make sure of that.

Now during the last spring assembly Jørgensen the sheriff's deputy held a sampling party that had got the guests to take their hats off to him. See, there is the real, until now undiscovered, Jørgensen! Not the least amazement was caused by Anga – simply a mistress – without acting the mistress of course in her housewife's dignity.

But otherwise Anga had turned into a quivering aspen leaf. Mostly he repressed her with his jealousy of the poor Mikkal; suspected and accused her of having one way or the other cajoled her way into the wine cellar to get hold of liquor for Mikkal – he seemed to have noticed it on one of the cognac bottles.

… One day in July, while little Olle and his father were building a little riverboat that Olle would have for his private use up there at the summer pasture, Jørgensen comes running, out of breath – yeah, whether Olle could run up to the summer pasture and get the midwife – he would get one krone for that. And hardly had he said it than Olle runs down to the river, shoves a boat out and poles over.

He hurries across the path through the pine moors there on the north side; the only time he took steps was when he had to go up over the steep wooded slope that led up from the headland … No, now his heart beats no more: he can run without stop – he had also had a pain in his chest this spring; but now he didn't feel a hint of it – runs, runs.

He had several times heard women in labor – oh, merciful God, how that was bad to hear! And now he is earning one krone! He runs and hums and yoiks about this krone. He did all to keep his sanity, while he ran through the wooded moor, on whose north side the high mountain knoll of pure rock-strewn slope went up. Inside that mountain lived the hill folk … it shook in his hair roots, and all of a sudden he had to cast a glance back and into the grove at the foot of the mountain.

He had run 12 miles non-stop when he got to the mountain summer farm. He barely got clabbered milk with sugar and milk finished and then sat in the back of the boat while the midwife rowed.

… But the worst was over when they came down to the village.

"You gave yourself too much time, Olle – you get no more than 50 øre, said Jørgensen."

Well, good grief! But Ville Jongo went with the 50 øre coin to Jørgensen and said that people weren't in the habit of being paid for wanting to help one nearest in a time of need.

And the midwife, a Sámi woman, got nothing – and besides it was not her damned duty to stay in the village for the entire time she knew that there were more pregnant women now.

… Later in the winter Jørgensen had gotten into a legal action with his father-in-law – he had accused Ågall of having cheated him, when Ågall last summer as the result of an assignment from his son-in-law had bought goods at an auction from a bankrupt businessman in a fishing station. And people were speechless with surprise that Jørgensen dared – and that Ågall seemed bewildered – just his owl eyes had sparkled uniquely. And already before Ågall had had to sit and eat in the kitchen when he was here and visited his daughter. The same had happened also to Anga's mother and sister last year and Anga had been told clearly that Jørgensen didn't want to have anything to do with her family. What good was it that old Ågall's owl eyes sparkled. But that Jørgensen nevertheless dared! People were almost in awe of him, admired him.

And sometimes Jørgensen was interim sheriff in his uncle's stead. One day before Christmas he was going to arrest the smith Balto Hansa who had gotten drunk and made a racket at a neighbor's farm. The smith protested, and when Jørgensen stuck his thumb into the smith's mouth and pulled the corner of the mouth to the side – to restrain the obstinate smith, Balto Hansa bit fast into the finger and didn't let go, although Jørgensen had gotten a strangle hold on him with his other hand. Balto Hansa bit and bit.

… It turned into blood poisoning – and Jørgensen had suddenly gotten so poorly that he himself couldn't travel down to the doctor in the closest fjord district, 110 miles from here – the doctor had to be fetched. Ågall had just come to the inland village, and he got permission to see his son-in-law, but Ågall didn't think he could accomplish anything in this case – as many miracles as he had otherwise done.

When the doctor arrived Jørgensen lay already unconscious. No, there was nothing to do; but one could perhaps waken the dying man to consciousness one more time by pouring a little champagne in him. Anga, his wife, looked at the pants hanging on the wall.

"But I don't dare take the keys, she said trembling and afraid for her life."

"I dare," said the sheriff's wife who was also present, and she took the keys out of Jørgensen's pants pocket and got a bottle of champagne from Jørgensen's holy wine cellar. They lifted the dying man up a little and poured champagne into him; he awoke – smacked his lips a little and then with his dulled eyes said suspiciously to his wife.

"Where did you get this champagne?" he asked.

Anga trembles and is silent.

"It is mine," said the sheriff's wife.

But then the dying man drew himself up and with an unpleasant expression on his face said:

"I ask one more time: where did you get this champagne?"

And he sank back and closed his eyes forever.

… Upset and beside herself Anga goes down into the wine cellar in the evening; she laughs hollowly and weirdly – speaks after the dead one: I ask one more time: where did you get this champagne? And one by one she crushes the bottles, saying every time: I ask one more time. And she wades in all this holy fluid on the floor.

◆

It was said a lot that Jørgensen ought not come onto consecrated ground; but on the other side, it was also true that he had not been guilty of perjury and such.

***

But during the autumn flood the year after one could tell that people had seen a man lying bound to a rather small timber raft floating down the river. Someone should have caught sight of this unpleasant timber raft already immediately below the village here; it rattled against splintering, newly formed ice – and floated down – and it was seen also by people in the solitary and small settlements there far down into the long valley. Always, always the raft with the man lying in it kept to the middle of the current – had danced in the night down the first large set of rapids below *Rastá Gáisá*. Continued down the 50 mile-long stretch; danced down the Big Chasm. Finally ended out in the fjord. Once out at sea the bands that had held the body and its soul fast on the little raft loosened; oh, if only they had loosened earlier!

… It was said that if someone wanted to dig up Jørgensen's grave, it would surely show that there was no body in the grave any longer – it lay at sea.

And Ågall's reputation began to climb anew. And that should have been known before – and the deceased should also have known … Ågall would not allow that sort of thing to remain sitting on himself. And no revenge is so indescribably unpleasant as that which befalls a person after death.

Árra geassi
Early Summer

Andijn had been south in the capital for a while, but had come home again. Down there the tall, beautiful woman with the bright golden hair could not go unnoticed; but that world there could somehow nevertheless not give her any feeling of home – not now any more. Could be that much would have developed otherwise for her, if she hadn't traveled down there with the ruins in her mind – after the earth tremor she had experienced.

Now and then she was with Fridtjof and Lisa in the little town on the fjord; but she always returned to the inland village here and did chores in the house of her parents.

Halle Johanas had gotten married and had both horse and river boat now. No, Andijn he didn't have to thank for that; but all the same he always carried with him a feeling of gratitude toward Andijn. He had run his good horse to death that time; but he now thought that the experience had been very valuable for him, put fertile soil in his heart. The boat he had lost in the Big Chasm because he couldn't bring himself to refuse to row Andijn ashore at the last moment – when she implored him to do it … no, he wouldn't do without that experience now; it was well worth a sacrifice. And Andijn that spring, while he was building the little log house on the riverbank, had come with the first pussy willows in her hand – and inside the log house she had tickled him on his bare, sunburned chest. But no one else knew about that – no, no one knew about that – it does good to be able to keep what is most precious to oneself.

And always, always Andijn came on a short visit to Halle Johanas and his wife, and always had something with her for their little child that she had also been a godmother for.

**

It was this that was so difficult for Hendrik Hooch to escape: when that evening, even before the letter from Einar Asper had come, and in which he had thought up excusing himself to Andijn because he feared that he had gotten a tumor on his brain, and therefore had to turn back – when Hendrik Hooch in his distress beforehand and purely accidentally had thought up telling Andijn that Einar Asper probably had a tumor on his brain and that there had been mental illness in his family. Who had put those words in his mouth!

And a half year later Hendrik Hooch got a message that Fridtjof, his own son, had had both of his eyeballs removed.

… But now Fridtjof in spite of everything had become a happy man. Who could know: whether that wasn't also a way of saving a life – from what could have been worse.

Otherwise, Hendrik Hooch and his wife had begun to resign themselves to the thought that it was in vain to ponder about what purpose it would serve that Einar Asper's energetic and dwindling soul had to live on Andijn's life-blood and take it along into death.

There was otherwise not much to notice about Andijn. It had to be that she one winter evening or another suddenly got into the habit of sitting and listening.

Maybe she was listening for sleigh bells – as she had done that evening – and it was as if she looked around for the lights that would be lit when Einar and the sleigh bell sound came nearer. It would be festively lighted over the whole estate and over the yard around.

But then she usually walked to Halle Johanas and got him to hitch up the horse and take her for a ride along the riverbend.

***

Matti Aikio – John Savio

The paths of two formidable Sámi artists may have crossed in Oslo or Tana in the 1920's. By then Aikio (b. 1872) had written many books and had been a journalist in Oslo for years. Savio, some 30 years younger, (b. 1902) was an up-and-coming, largely self-taught artist best known for his woodcuts. Both faced nearly insurmountable obstacles in their lives including financial woes and tuberculosis; Aikio died at 56, Savio 36. More importantly, both lived during the era of social Darwinism and the harsh assimilation of the Sámi in Norway. Aikio did not begin to study Norwegian until he was 18, yet he spent his entire career away from his home area writing articles and books in a language that was not his mother tongue. Savio lost his entire family before he turned 3 and was raised by his grandparents. Moreover, as Sámi artists both men were going against the grain: the concept "art for art's sake" did not exist in Sámi. Everything made had to have utilitarian value: a novel or a woodcut did not put bread on the table. Sámi *duodji* or handicrafts could be made artistically but had to be useful. The word *dáidda* for art did not become current until the 1970's. So Aikio and Savio were doing something not valued by most Sámi at that time. Aikio was writing novels about the exotic indigenous people who lived in the far north, exactly what a broad Norwegian public was hungry for. However, many Sámi considered it a betrayal of their culture. Aikio felt like *geasat*, a reindeer calf born in summer, i.e., one who does not fit in. But in Oslo Aikio kept his Sámi name and wore his Sámi costume, so it is not surprising that he pushed for the right of his people to their own culture, something that became a reality for the Sámi many years later. Savio too was a champion of Sámi causes: his life motto was "to show the world the Sámi people" and describe a way of life on the verge of being lost. Aikio, keenly interested in sculpture, published a book on the Norwegian sculptor Gustav Vigeland in 1920; he considered Vigeland to be one of the greatest of all time and on a par with Rodin. Aikio debuted as a sculptor himself in 1926, but when he saw Savio's graphic work he is supposed to have said: "He will become a world famous artist." Aikio went on to write *Borgere og nomader* which came out shortly after his death as *Bygden på Elvenesset*.

Made in the USA
Lexington, KY
15 February 2018